He li█████████████████████his, all soft
and v███████████████████

That s█████████████████████ under his
watch shifted something in his chest. He'd never
met a woman like Olivia. Whatever he was feeling
toward her, he wanted it to last.

The urge to climb into that bed with her and
make love was powerful. No sooner than he
settled in next to her did she start to flail and cry
out. She was having another nightmare.

"Olivia." He shook her gently, but she fought him
off. "Olivia, wake up."

Her eyes flew open and she screamed.

"Olivia, it's me. It's okay. You were dreaming."

She blinked, inhaled a ragged breath and scrambled
away from him. Her eyes looked crazed when she
looked at him. "Bad things happened there, Russ.
Things we don't even know yet."

Dear Reader,

The first Colby Agency book, *Safe by His Side,* was released by Harlequin Intrigue in September 2000. Time has flown and the stories featuring Victoria Colby and her esteemed team of private investigators have stolen my heart.

You journeyed with Victoria through the painful memories of having lost her first husband and her son. You held your breath as her son returned a broken man determined to take his life back. You cheered for Victoria when she allowed herself to put the past behind her and love Lucas Camp, the man who had been there for her through it all. You have shared the danger as evil has tried repeatedly to destroy the Colbys and the triumphs of new love and the birth of children and grandchildren.

Most important, you have taken this journey with me every step of the way. I cannot thank you enough for helping me to make the Colby family a great success. As I faced my own personal challenges, your outpouring of support and concern has helped me rise above the pain and defeat it to write that next story and to keep believing in myself and the work. Please know that I read every letter and email that you sent. I look forward to many, many more years of writing the stories I love and sharing those journeys with you. I hope you enjoy this fiftieth Colby Agency story. Never fear, more Colbys are on the way!

Very best!

Debra Webb

DEBRA WEBB

COLBY ROUNDUP

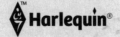

TORONTO NEW YORK LONDON
AMSTERDAM PARIS SYDNEY HAMBURG
STOCKHOLM ATHENS TOKYO MILAN MADRID
PRAGUE WARSAW BUDAPEST AUCKLAND

Recycling programs
for this product may
not exist in your area.

ISBN-13: 978-0-373-69626-0

COLBY ROUNDUP

ABOUT THE AUTHOR

Debra Webb wrote her first story at age nine and her first romance at thirteen. It wasn't until she spent three years working for the military behind the Iron Curtain and within the confining political walls of Berlin, Germany, that she realized her true calling. A five-year stint with NASA on the space-shuttle program reinforced her love of the endless possibilities within her grasp as a storyteller. A collision course between suspense and romance was set. Debra has been writing romance, suspense and action-packed romance thrillers since. Visit her at www.debrawebb.com or write to her at P.O. Box 4889, Huntsville, AL 35815.

Books by Debra Webb

CAST OF CHARACTERS

Russell St. James—As a former cop, Russ knows his way around an investigation, but everything about this case is different. How do you protect a woman who doesn't realize she's in danger?

Olivia Westfield—Olivia has just learned she was adopted and that her biological parents are convicted serial killers. But what if one or both is innocent? With her legal background, Olivia intends to find the truth.

Rafe and Clare Barker—The Princess Killers. Which of them is really the cold-blooded murderer? The one on death row or the one recently released?

Tony Weeden—Who is he loyal to? Rafe? Clare? Or himself?

Janet Tolliver—She held the key to many dark, dangerous secrets….

Victoria Colby-Camp—She and Lucas are supposed to be retired, but there is something about this case that just won't let them go. After Lucas almost lost his life to this heinous case, Victoria is even more determined that they retire.

Lucas Camp—He fears Victoria is being drawn into an emotional war that will tear her apart.

Simon Ruhl—The head of the new Colby, Texas, agency.

Chapter One

Polunsky Prison, Polk County Texas,
Monday, June 3, 3:00 p.m.

Olivia Westfield paced the stark interview room to which she had been sequestered. She paused long enough to take a breath and reminded herself that she needed to remain calm. Any visible sign of anticipation or anxiety would be a mistake. Though she was not an attorney, she had sat in enough courtrooms with her boss, who was the best criminal attorney in San Antonio, to know how to lead a witness, especially a potential hostile witness. During the next few minutes, it was immensely important that she lead.

It had taken her a week to get this interview, and then the warden had only been persuaded by her boss's connection to an esteemed Texas senator with the right amount of clout. The prisoner Olivia was here to see was the most infamous death row inmate in Texas's history. Since she was not his attorney, the interview had been extremely difficult to secure. The opportunity both terrified and exhilarated her.

Raymond Rafe Barker had spent twenty-two years in prison, seventeen on death row. In all those years he had not provided the locations of all the missing bodies of his many alleged victims, including those of his three young daughters. In a mere seventeen days he would be executed by lethal injection for his alleged heinous crimes. Olivia wanted his story—the whole story.

But what if he was innocent?

The tangle of nerves that had been twisting inside her for days tightened to a hard knot. Was she making a mistake doing this? Revealing herself to the man who could very well change the course of the rest of her life? Only her boss knew the reason for her need to meet the convicted murderer and learn the real story of what happened all those years ago in a small Texas community. Eventually the world would know; it was inevitable. The ramifications were immense, the impact potentially widespread.

Mistake or not, ultimately she had to do this. Whatever the consequences, living the rest of her life without knowing the truth was something she simply could not do. The past twenty-plus years of her life had been built on too many deceptions. From this moment forward she wanted the truth, the whole truth and nothing but. Want didn't begin to describe what Olivia felt. She *needed* the truth; she needed answers.

The door of the interview room opened. Olivia snapped from her disturbing thoughts. She mentally and physically braced for the impact of meeting the man who was a convicted serial murderer, a coldhearted sociopath according to the law. An inmate who had maintained his silence all this time as to what really happened so many years ago. This man, who held the key to those answers, was also her biological father.

That reality stole her breath yet again.

Two prison guards escorted Rafe Barker into the room. The leg irons around his ankles and the belly chain coiled about his waist rattled as he was ushered to a chair at the table in the center of the small interview room. One of the two chairs stationed around the table was drawn back.

"Sit," one of the guards ordered.

Unable to drag in a gulp of air even now, Olivia watched

the prisoner's every move. He hadn't looked at her yet. She wasn't sure how to feel about that or the possibility of whether or not he would recognize her, for that matter.

It had been twenty-two years since he'd last seen her.

For God's sake, what had she been thinking coming here?

Barker glanced at the guard on his left, then followed the instruction to be seated. He settled into the molded plastic chair. The second guard secured the leg irons to the floor and the ones binding Barker's hands to his waist to the underside of the sturdy table.

"We'll be just outside, Ms. Westfield," the first guard said to Olivia. "Just knock on the door when you're finished here." He shot a glance at the man he obviously considered a monster before meeting her gaze once more.

"Thank you." Her voice was a little shaky and she regretted that outward demonstration of apprehension. *Be strong, Liv.*

When the door had closed behind the guards, Olivia drew in a deep, steadying breath and crossed to the table. She sat down and met the gaze of the man now studying her intently. From what she understood he spent twenty-three hours per day confined to his cell and it showed in the pale skin stretched across his gaunt face; a face that narrowed down to slumped shoulders and a rail-thin body covered by generic prison garb. But the most startling aspect of his appearance was the faded brown eyes. Eyes that perhaps had once been the more vivid chocolate color of hers. The high cheekbones and slim nose were as familiar as the reflection she considered in the mirror each morning.

Genetically speaking, this was her father. No question. No doubts. Her heart pounded with the rush of emotions she couldn't quite define. Anger, defeat, regret…one, or all, maybe.

"Why are you here?" he asked.

The rustiness of his voice made her flinch. His speech

croaked with disuse and age that belied his true years. The warden had told her that Barker rarely spoke to anyone. He had refused to grant a single interview with reporters or cold-case investigators or to cooperate with the doctors who'd attempted to analyze him during the past two decades.

His question—four little words—churned those already turbulent emotions, making her quake inside with a vulnerability she wanted desperately to deny. "That's a good question." She cleared the rasp of uncertainty from her own voice. "I suppose I felt compelled to see you before it was too late."

In seventeen days he would be dead. More of those troubling emotions stirred deep in her belly. Emotions she shouldn't feel for a stranger…a convicted killer. The faint idea that he might not be guilty toyed with her desire for justice…for hope that he was not that heinous monster.

"Do you know who I am?" he ventured, his eyes searching hers for any indication of what she was thinking beyond her vague response. Obviously he felt something, curiosity maybe. Was it even possible for him to feel anything else?

This man who had been labeled pure evil was her *father*. Dear God. He *was* her father. Sitting face-to-face with him, she could not deny that glaring fact. Part of her had wanted to latch onto the idea that it could be a mistake. The photos she had seen from the trial more than twenty years ago had not adequately prepared her for *this*. She hadn't seen him like this, in person, since she was five years old. Basically, she remembered nothing from that time…except in her dreams.

As far back as she could recall, the nightmares had haunted her sleep. The screaming…the blood. The darkness and then the soothing humming—a tune she hadn't been able to identify. Not that she'd really tried. She shook off the images and sounds that tried to intrude even now. Her adoptive parents had blamed the images and sounds on a scary movie she'd watched with a cousin. Another of their well-meant deceptions.

So many, many lies.

"I know who you are." She clasped her hands in her lap to prevent him from seeing the shaking that had overtaken her body. As hard as she tried, she couldn't make it stop. Good thing she wasn't in a courtroom right now. Prosecutors ate nervous defense attorneys and their assistants for breakfast.

Raymond Barker was the Princess Killer. The man charged and convicted of the murders of more than a dozen young girls. The man who had been charged with murdering his own daughters. That was the real reason Olivia was here. She'd had no choice in the matter. The media had gotten it wrong. The police who investigated the murders had gotten it wrong.

Olivia was this man's daughter. If Rafe Barker hadn't killed her, was it possible he hadn't killed anyone? Made sense that if she was alive, her sisters would be, too. She needed an answer to that, as well. Olivia had studied the case. She knew the details, at least the ones that had played out in the media. She had interviewed the detectives who investigated the case, but she had not been allowed to see the actual case files. The detective who'd been in charge, Marcus Whitt, had told her straight up that he didn't appreciate her nosing around.

Giving herself grace, she had only just learned the identity of her biological parents two weeks ago. Before she'd gotten to the point of actually moving forward, Clare Barker had been released from prison—her conviction overturned—and that had changed everything in her opinion. Olivia had tried unsuccessfully to find her.

Her mother. The woman who had professed her innocence for more than two decades. If she was innocent, why hadn't she come to Olivia? Had she contacted the other two women? Sarah, who had been named Sadie by her adoptive parents, and Lisa, named Laney by the folks who adopted her? Olivia had no idea where her sisters were but she intended to find them. The three of them needed to face this challenge together. Time was running out and desperation had lodged deep in her soul.

But what if her sisters didn't know? Olivia's adoptive parents had kept their secret for twenty-two years. As much as she loved the people who had raised her, that decision had been the wrong one. She should have known the truth long ago. What if her sisters didn't want to know? Was it fair for her to impose her personal quest upon their lives?

Rafe cleared his throat, the saggy muscles there working as if the words he intended to utter were difficult to impart. "Whatever you believe about me, I'm thankful you came."

The air she struggled to draw in trapped beneath her breastbone. The ache it generated made speaking as hard for her as it appeared to have been for him. "I need you to tell me the truth about what happened when I was a child."

The prospect carried monumental implications even beyond the potential added pain to the families of the victims. Her chest tightened at the conceivability of what his long-awaited words might mean for all those damaged hearts... what they might mean for her. For her sisters...women she didn't even know.

He had refused to talk from the moment he and his wife— Clare, her mother—were arrested. Today, he had just over two weeks to live. Why not tell the world the truth? Unless, of course, the truth was that he, in fact, was the heinous killer society thought him to be.

Clare Barker had relentlessly stood by her story that she was innocent. According to what Olivia had gleaned, as the investigation of the case had progressed, the bodies of eight young girls, ranging in age from twelve to seventeen, had been recovered but several others remained unaccounted for. Clare insisted that she knew nothing about any of the abductions or the murders. Both Clare and Rafe had been respected members of the community of Granger. No one had suspected either of the slightest legal infraction…yet numerous sets of remains had been exhumed from the woods just beyond their own backyard. A backyard where their daughters, including Olivia, had played.

The reality of that fact made her sick to her stomach. But who was the killer and who was the oblivious bystander? Someone was lying, because Olivia was alive. That had to mean one story or the other was wrong, at least to a degree.

He studied her for a long moment with those too-familiar brown eyes. "The truth you seek will not ease the torment your soul suffers, I fear." He looked down as if he also feared his eyes would give away his true thoughts.

How dare he make such a statement! His suggestion that he had even the most remote concept of what she might think or feel infuriated her. "What about all those other families who want nothing more than to bury their dead? Will you take your secrets to your grave and twist the dagger once more?" She shook her head. "Maybe you are the monster they say you are. Whether you are or not, the truth can't hurt you now. But it could help others." Including her. Her whole life felt out of sync.

He inhaled a sharp breath. "I'm no monster. What I am is a fool. I slept in the bed with her every night and never had the vaguest idea what she was doing right under my nose. I don't deserve to live. My blindness is inexcusable." The craggy features of his face tightened as he visibly fought for composure. "I can't do a thing to bring those girls back and I don't know that the truth, if I had it to give you, would comfort their families. Dead is dead. The only good thing I accomplished was to get the three of you to safety. I wanted you to have a normal life. I didn't want my legacy to haunt your life." He moved his head side to side. "That may be impossible now. You shouldn't have come here. You took too great a risk."

Her fury exploded with a ferocity she could scarcely contain. "How can you pretend to know what's best for me? You have no idea who I am. What about the others? My sisters. Where are they?"

"They're alive and well," he assured her. "Whatever you believe," he said, his eyes watery, "my only concern is for your continued safety. That's why I called the Colby Agency. They're supposed to be protecting my girls."

This announcement startled her, momentarily shoved aside the fury and the tangle of emotions funneling inside her. "What're you talking about?" She'd sensed someone following her the past few days but she hadn't spotted anyone. Finally, she'd decided it was her imagination. With the life-altering discoveries she'd made over the past fourteen days, she couldn't trust her judgment or her instincts. "There's no one protecting me." She was perfectly capable of protecting herself.

"The only thing I ever wanted was for the three of you to be safe and happy." The sadness in his eyes looked convincing enough. "She would've killed you, too. I made sure you were out of her reach. Until now. When her sentence was overturned, I had to do something. I reached out to the only people I felt could be trusted. The Colby Agency. Their reputation speaks for itself."

A barrage of questions whirled like a cyclone inside her head. "I haven't heard from any Colby Agency." How could he sit there and pretend to care about her welfare?

"They're watching you," he promised. "Protecting you from her. Her release is the only reason I broke my silence."

Don't get distracted, Olivia. Don't let him lead. Read between the lines. "You're saying you're innocent, but unless you have proof of that claim—"

He shook his head again. "Don't need any proof. I'm reconciled to my fate. It's nothing more than I deserve for being a fool. As long as my girls are safe that's all that matters to me. I can leave this world satisfied."

His suggestion that Clare would come after her daughters with malicious intent stretched the boundaries of credibility. "Why would she do this? Clare, I mean. She's free. No one can touch her now." She had nothing to gain and everything to lose.

He leaned forward. Olivia instinctively reared back before she could prevent the reaction. "She will do anything to hurt me. When she figured out I'd hidden the three of you away, she began her battle to gain her freedom. Took her twenty-some years, but she did it. Now none of you are safe with her free."

"If she's trying to get to me, she's not very good at it." Maybe Clare had been following her instead of the Colby Agency. Could a woman in her mid-fifties fresh on the street from an extended death-row confinement be that stealthy?

"If you believe nothing else," he warned, "believe me when I say she will find a way. You're the oldest. Find your sisters. The Colby Agency knows where they are. Do what you can to help keep them safe…like you used to do."

Olivia went completely still inside. More of those images and sounds from her dreams surfaced.

"Don't let her do what she tried to do when you were babies. She's evil. Pure evil, Olivia. She won't stop until you're all dead and I'm in hell where she wanted me all along."

Chapter Two

Russell St. James waited well outside the long entry and gate that barred admittance to Polunsky Prison. He'd left his car a considerable distance from the entrance to avoid being spotted by Olivia Westfield, aka Olivia Barker. Based on her movements the past twelve days, she clearly sensed she was being followed. He'd had to take extreme care with his surveillance. The woman was no fool. At least, he'd thought she wasn't until now.

This latest move was troubling. He'd already informed Victoria Colby-Camp and Simon Ruhl, head of the Colby Agency's Houston office. All were braced for the impact of what Olivia's visit to Rafe Barker might mean.

She had no idea the kind of danger she was in. Clare Barker and her apparent partner were now wanted as persons of interest in the murder of the ex-boyfriend of Laney Seagers, aka Lisa Barker. As well as the attempted murders of both Lucas Camp and Colby investigator Joel Hayden. Clare's partner, Tony Weeden, would likely be deemed the prime suspect in that ongoing investigation any time now. The two were also under investigation for the abduction of Laney's five-year-old son. Though the boy's father, Laney's ex-boyfriend Terrence Kingston, took the boy initially, Clare and Weeden grabbed him after the murder. The unknown variable was which of the two committed the murder. The likelihood of Kingston having been murdered before Clare and Weeden found him was highly unlikely since the child had survived the event. This was a very dangerous scenario and growing more dangerous with each passing day.

The actions of Clare and Weeden indicated a building level of desperation. That was never good. The two were obviously capable of anything and the Colby Agency could only guess at the ultimate goal of one or both.

Russ's initial assignment had been to watch Olivia while keeping his distance. Disrupting her life had not been on his agenda. That had changed now. The risk was too great to remain at a distance. Depending on the outcome of Olivia's abrupt visit to her father, which the agency had only confirmed was going down two hours ago, Russ was prepared to intercept Olivia and spell it all out for her. She knew more than her sisters had. Neither Laney nor youngest sister Sadie Gilmore, aka Sarah Barker, had known they were adopted.

Yesterday, Russ had followed Olivia from her home in San Antonio to just outside Livingston. She'd spent the night in a modest motel with the briefcase and one small bag she'd carried into her room. He'd gotten the adjoining room and spent several hours listening to her cell phone conversation with her boss, attorney Nelson Belden. The lady had discovered about two weeks ago that the Barkers were her biological parents. That part saved Russ the uncomfortable task of relating the news. The other side of that scenario was that she appeared bent on finding the truth about the Princess murders.

Russ removed his hat and ran a hand through his hair before settling the Stetson back in place. No question that all three of the Barker girls deserved the truth. Trouble was, right now was not a good time to start digging into the past. At least not until the danger was under control.

Denying the lady had an understandable agenda wasn't possible. She had just learned her existence up to now was built on a foundation of untruths. Equally understandable was her adoptive parents' reasons for keeping the ugliness of the past from her, at least in the early years. Based on the conversation he'd overheard last night Olivia was on the outs with the folks who had raised her over the well-kept secret. Oddly, she hadn't mentioned this visit in the conversation with her boss. Whether she'd been waiting for approval or keeping it from Belden, which didn't add up, was yet to be seen. Whatever she hoped to gain with a face-to-face with Rafe Barker, Russ feared she would be vastly disappointed.

This was a volatile state of affairs and after her meeting with Barker it was only going to grow more unpredictable.

The cell phone in his hip pocket vibrated. He dragged it out and accepted the call from his boss, Simon Ruhl. "St. James."

"A doctor's office in Brenham was broken into early this morning. We believe Weeden may have been involved since the items taken would be useful for his gunshot injury and his white sedan was found in the area. We're hoping to get a confirmation from the prints lifted at the scene. Neither he nor Clare has been spotted in the area and we have no reports of stolen vehicles. Either the two are laying low nearby or have *borrowed* a vehicle that the owner hasn't yet reported missing. Judging by the distance and direction traveled, we feel he and Clare may be headed back to the Houston area or perhaps to Livingston."

"I assume that means I should intercept Ms. Westfield and lay out the situation." Sounded like the next step to Russ. Waiting any longer would only make his job more challenging. He needed to be as close to Olivia as feasible, particularly if Clare and Weeden were headed for her. The two had attempted contact with Sadie and Laney. Logic dictated that a crack at interacting with Olivia would be next.

The trouble was no one on the Colby team could guess the motive. If a simple reunion was the goal, why go about it so covertly and with the collateral damage of the past few days? From the fire at Clare's apartment building in Copperas Cove shortly after her release, to her activities related to connecting with her two younger daughters, not the least of which was kidnaping the Laney's son, a simple, peaceful reunion appeared to be the last thing on the woman's mind.

"Keep your distance until she reaches her next destination," Simon advised, hauling Russ from the worrisome musings. "Move in at that point. We need to see where she plans on taking this new step. I'll keep you informed of what we learn here."

"Will do." Russ tucked his phone back into his pocket. He took one last look at the ominous gray buildings that represented the Polunsky Prison unit where Texas's male death row inmates resided until their number was up.

He hoped Olivia understood that the man inside those walls was capable of most anything at this point. Though it appeared Weeden was working with Clare and represented the biggest threat, in reality, Weeden had served as a prison nurse and Rafe Barker had been one of his patients. The two had apparently formed a bond. It was not outside the realm of possibility that Weeden was following a plan he and Rafe had devised and Clare was nothing more than a foolish pawn. The psychiatric analysis from her prison medical records indicated the woman was not genius material but she was of average intelligence. Despite a college education, Clare Barker had been a simple woman. One whose neighbors had once thought to be kind and generous. Nothing in her psych evaluations suggested serious mental deficiencies. Withdrawn, secretive, with glimmers of paranoia. Nothing overtly violent or dramatic.

But that didn't make her innocent. It made her a total unknown variable with an agenda that somehow involved her daughters. If Rafe could be believed, she wanted all three dead before his execution just to spite him.

Bottom line, Rafe was the one with nothing to lose. In seventeen days he would be dead. Russ hoped his goal was not to take his daughters with him using Weeden or Clare or both. And the Colby Agency.

Whether it was Rafe or Clare who represented the threat, the situation was building and an explosion was inevitable.

Russ returned to the residence where he'd parked his SUV and waited, thankful that no one was home to question his hanging out in their driveway. Every advantage was crucial.

Using compact binoculars, Russ watched the prison's entry gate. He didn't have to wait long until the towering blockade moved to allow a single vehicle to exit. Tan sedan. Olivia Westfield was coming out.

"What're you going to do now, little lady?" he murmured.

Russ put the binoculars aside and started his SUV. He'd give her a few seconds' head start and then he'd follow. A tracking device tucked beneath her rear bumper prevented any real concern about losing her. The device fed to his cell, providing her every turn as long as he didn't allow too much distance between them. As a former Dallas cop, he'd done his share of surveillance duty. He had to admit, this was the first time he'd been detailed to watch a person of interest before the crime occurred. Most of his experience had been clocked tracking down criminals, not protecting the innocent before a threat was identified and confirmed.

He pulled out onto Farm to Market Road with her in the distance but still visible. Since she hadn't taken her suitcase from the motel, it was a safe bet that she would return there at some point in the evening.

The distance between their vehicles diminished and he slowed accordingly. As she continued to slow a frown furrowed an annoying path across his brow. Her driving pattern thus far had been relatively fast and furious but she apparently didn't want another speeding ticket like yesterday, because she was driving well under the speed limit.

Following her lead, Russ slowed again. What was she up to? Was she forcing him to draw closer and closer?

Then she sped up. He applied a little more pressure to the accelerator to avoid the gap between them from widening beyond a comfortable span. She surged forward, moving well past the posted speed limit. Apparently she wasn't concerned about another speeding ticket, after all.

No more speculating, she knew he was tailing her and she wanted him to know it. Fortunately the highway was deserted save for the two of them. If the lady wanted to outdrive him she was going to have to do better than this. Flooring the accelerator, he urged his SUV forward, preserving a visual on the tan sedan. His grip tightened on the steering wheel as he barreled along the road in her wake. There was no traffic for her to get lost in…no turns onto crowded streets. Just open road and the question of who would give in to the inevitable first.

Red flashed a warning. *Brake lights.* His right foot went instinctively to the brake pedal, applying considerable pressure without sending his SUV fishtailing.

She hit her brakes again, harder this time. The sedan slid to a screaming crossways stop in the road.

He rammed his brake harder, burning rubber to a stop some three or four feet from the driver's-side door. She was out of the car and stalking toward him before he'd shifted into Park.

The lady was not happy.

Russ climbed out, keeping his movements slow and steady. She wasn't armed with firepower but she carried a canister that he suspected was pepper spray or some other unpleasant deterrent he would prefer to avoid.

"Who the hell are you?" She stopped well within range of showering him with the weapon she wielded. As if she was considering acting first and getting answers later, the fingers of her right hand tightened around the black canister.

Holding up his hands in the classic gesture of surrender, Russ offered her a congenial smile. "May I remove my ID and show you?" A smart lady wouldn't simply take his word for it. And this one was definitely smart.

Her gaze narrowed with suspicion. "Answer the question. Who are you?" she repeated, not giving an inch and certainly not smiling. She intended that he do this her way. Smart and sassy.

"Russ St. James. I'm with the Colby Agency, a private investigations firm out of Houston." No reason to complicate the matter with details. Simon had given him the authorization to approach, not that he'd needed it as it turned out.

The suspicion didn't fade completely but she visibly relaxed her battle-ready stance. "I'd like to see that ID now."

Russ removed his wallet from his hip pocket and held it out to her. "Be my guest. Make a call if you need confirmation."

She inched close enough to snatch the wallet from his fingers. Her chin-length blondish-brown hair fell around her face as she opened his wallet and studied his credentials. Her hair a little darker than sister Laney's, the lush brown color was accentuated with strands of gold, giving her hair a sheen most women paid big bucks for at their favorite salons. But not the Barker girls. Sadie, the youngest, was blonder than her older sisters. They all had lavish, eye-catching manes that even cut as short as Olivia's would not be ignored. All but Sadie had deep, rich brown eyes. Whatever warped genes carried by one or both their parents, the girls had gotten all the best traits in the looks department. All three were smart and independent.

Unlike her younger sisters, Olivia was a white-collar professional, a paralegal at a prestigious San Antonio law firm, with a wardrobe that shouted success. No jeans and cowgirl boots for her. Elegant pencil skirts and spiked high heels all the way. As conservative as her taste in clothing appeared to be with those long skirts and high-collar blouses, the way the fabric molded to her figure rocked with sensuality.

"You needn't waste any more of your time." She shoved the wallet back at him. "I don't need your protection, Mr. St. James. I can take care of myself."

Russ accepted his wallet and tucked it away. Seemed Rafe Barker had told her about his request for protection from the Colby Agency; otherwise, she would certainly have had more questions. "We should talk about that before you make your decision, Ms. Westfield," he suggested.

She shook her head, folded her arms over her chest in finality. "I'm afraid that would be impossible. I'm not at liberty to discuss a case I'm investigating with you or anyone else."

His instincts perked up. "You're looking into the Princess Killer case? If so, I definitely have information you need to consider before moving forward."

Those brown eyes narrowed once more. "I'm relatively certain you don't have anything I don't already know. I appreciate the offer, but I have things to do." She squared her shoulders. "If you persist in following me, I will have no choice but to take out a restraining order. So back off."

Well, there was that. Russ had one ace up his sleeve. "I have something for you that may facilitate your investigation. If you're willing to give me a few minutes of your time, we can—"

Her eyebrows raised in blatant speculation. "I did an internet search of your agency before driving out of the prison parking lot. I wouldn't have thought an investigator from such an esteemed agency would carry around blackmail in his bag of tricks. If you had something of interest you surely would have said that up front. We're done here, Mr. St. James."

"Ms. Westfield," Russ said, reaching for patience, "I'm not the enemy. Mr. Barker sought out my agency to protect you. I would be remiss if I didn't at least attempt to satisfy his request."

"Fine. Let's not waste more time. What is it you have that you believe will interest me?"

Nothing like getting straight to the point. "I have a photo album from…" How did he explain? "From your early childhood. There are newspaper clippings related to the Barkers' arrest and trial, as well."

A car rolled up, drawing their attention to the road behind her sedan. Russ tensed. Gray in color. Four doors. Two occupants in the front seat. One male, one female. The driver's-side window powered down. Russ's right hand went instinctively to the small of his back where his weapon rested. Clare and her accomplice, Weeden, could be watching Olivia the same as he was.

The driver, the male, poked his head out. *Not Weeden.* "You folks need any assistance?"

"We're fine. Thank you." Olivia moved toward her sedan. "I must have hit a slick spot in the road."

The man nodded, powered his window back up and drove around, using the shoulder of the road to avoid her front bumper.

Olivia glanced back at Russ. "Follow me."

Before he could ask where to she climbed back into her car and started the engine. Russ did the same. Just his luck. Ms. Westfield was going to make his job even more difficult than he'd anticipated. All he had to do was stay one step ahead of her excuses for not needing him.

Five seconds later they were exceeding the speed limit and heading to her destination of choice.

Chapter Three

Victoria Colby-Camp considered the curtains in her new living room. The small beach cottage half an hour from Houston had been a whirlwind weekend purchase. On Saturday, she'd left Lucas resting in the Beaumont hospital and viewed the cottage her Realtor had called about. She and Lucas had leased a condo several months ago and had been happy there while they searched for a permanent home in the Houston area.

The timing of the call from her Realtor had been perfect. Since Christmas last year she and Lucas had been waffling about the decision to retire completely. This investigation had made up Victoria's mind for her. Lucas had almost lost his life just three days ago. She would not allow that to happen again. It was time they moved on and focused forward.

The main Colby Agency offices in Chicago were in good hands with her son Jim and Ian Michaels, a long time second in command for Victoria. Simon Ruhl, another of her seconds in command, had relocated his wife and children to Houston and had the Texas office well underway. It was no longer necessary for her or for Lucas to be involved with the daily operations. They had often talked about taking a winter home. Actually, the plan was to spend as much time at one as the other, depending on the weather and circumstances with the grandchildren.

Victoria smiled as she thought of her grandchildren spending weeks on end with her and Lucas here on the beach. This choice was the perfect balance. Once she had seen this lovely cottage, she had returned to the hospital in Beaumont with pictures for Lucas. He agreed that it was the perfect second home. The transaction had been a simple matter at that point.

Since the cottage was furnished there was no reason not to move in immediately. She'd brought Lucas here this morning upon his release from the hospital. Victoria wandered over to the French doors that overlooked the terrace. She smiled as she watched her husband flip through the morning paper. He looked right at home lounging in that comfortable chaise. The bandage on his forehead would be gone soon. He would be wearing the walking cast for several more weeks. The sling for his arm wouldn't be necessary for quite so long. Thankfully his shoulder would heal without surgery. She felt certain that good fortune was wholly related to how very physically fit he remained when most men his age fell victim to sedentary work and activities. Not Lucas. He was strong and healthy. Despite the loss of his left leg during that awful war so many years ago, he had never allowed the awkwardness of a prosthesis to keep him from a fitness regimen. She wanted him to stay that way so they could enjoy their golden years together and with their growing family. Now that Slade, Lucas's son, and Maggie were married and had their precious baby girl, they would be visiting, as well. Slade would enjoy the quiet solitude here. His life had been challenging until now.

Beyond the patio and a small landscaped patch of lawn, the dazzling water lapped at the sandy shore only yards from their back door. Yes, she decided, they would be happy here. Victoria turned around in the spacious room. She adored the open floor plan. There was some redecorating to do. The furnishings weren't precisely suited to her and Lucas's taste, but that would be easily remedied in time. Those decisions could wait until they could shop together.

The sound of her cell chiming disrupted her leisurely daydreaming. Her heart stumbled into an awkward gallop. Though she knew Joel Hayden was well on his way to a complete recovery and safe with Laney Seagers and her son, Buddy, worry tugged at her. Sadie Gilmore and Lyle McCaleb were safe and making wedding plans. But Olivia Westfield remained in a place that was far too precarious. Simon had relayed the news to Victoria that Olivia had garnered a meeting with Rafe Barker, her biological father. This call might be regarding that meeting, which could prove detrimental to the agency's attempts to keep all three of the Barker girls safe. Olivia would be the most challenging. Her background in the legal field indicated she never settled for the status quo.

Knowing she could not ignore the call, Victoria moved across the room and picked up her cell. Simon's name appeared on the screen with the next chime.

"Good afternoon, Simon." She held her breath and hoped the rest of the afternoon wasn't about to be launched into chaos.

"How is Lucas handling a quiet day at home?" Simon inquired.

Disturbing news. Whenever Simon avoided a simple greeting and moved directly into neutral territory, he was preparing to deliver a less-than-pleasant update.

"He's skimming through the paper, having a drink fitting a leisurely afternoon on the beach. I should snap a photo and send it to you. I'm certain you would be amused. Do you have news about Olivia?" Victoria placed a hand on the island counter and held her breath.

"Warden Prentice indicated that nothing Barker said to

Olivia was new. He urged her to find her sisters and informed her that he had hired the agency to provide protection."

Victoria tried unsuccessfully to restrain the fury that sparked to life inside her. Rafe knew far more than he was sharing and his insistence on keeping aspects of the past to himself greatly hindered the agency's efforts. He was playing a game, she was convinced.

"What was Olivia's reaction?" Victoria could only imagine the emotional state the young woman was in since learning the news that her parents were not her birth parents and, even worse, that her biological parents were convicted murderers. She could not be in a rational place, making her far more susceptible to the danger circling the three Barker girls.

"St. James hasn't been able to gauge her reaction as of yet. Olivia confronted him shortly after leaving the prison and as we speak they're having a sit-down in a café in Livingston."

"Let me know as soon as you have an update from Russ." Victoria would feel much better when Olivia was reconciled to having round-the-clock protection.

"There's another development, Victoria. If I didn't know how much you want this case solved in a timely manner—" he sighed "—I wouldn't even pass this information on to you. With Lucas's injuries, I know your attention is needed there. But I am all too aware of your feelings on this case."

The hair on the back of her neck stood on end. This was the part she had sensed was coming. "I'm listening."

"Barker wants another meeting with you. Tomorrow morning, nine o'clock. He says he has additional information he is now prepared to share but he will only share it with you. I pushed the issue of taking the meeting personally but he refused."

Equal measures anticipation and anger fired along her nerves. "If this information is so compelling, why can't he share it now? Today? I can be in Livingston in a couple of hours." The bastard liked playing games with her. With all of them. Whether he was innocent of the crimes with which he was charged or not, he was a twisted soul.

"He refused to negotiate his terms. Nine tomorrow morning, you and you alone. What should I tell the warden?"

Victoria wished she could tell Barker to go to hell. She trusted nothing he said. But her hands were tied. No risk could be taken until they ascertained the true source of the danger to these women. "Tell him I'll be there."

"I'll accompany you," Simon offered.

"No. I can do this alone. Your efforts are needed elsewhere."

"Very well. I'll let Warden Prentice know to expect you."

Victoria ended the call and set her phone aside. She moved back to the French doors and watched her husband fold the paper and set it aside. Part of her wanted to simply stay right here and bar the world from her door. But that was impossible. Lucas would never run away from a challenge any more than she would. Her emotions made her vulnerable just now.

More than twenty-five years ago her son had been taken from her by one of the most evil men who had ever lived. He had tortured and brainwashed Jim for nearly two decades. If Rafe was lying, he had taken Clare's children from her and ensured she was charged for his heinous crimes right along with him. Victoria knew how that kind of loss and betrayal felt.

Yet Clare's actions since her release went against the idea that she was innocent and deserving of a reunion with her daughters. Victoria needed to ferret out the truth here. To reunite this family if possible.

She could not walk away until that was done.

Eventually the case would be solved one way or the other and her emotions would settle down. She would feel herself again. She and Lucas were safe and the Colby team investigating this case would be triumphant. Until then, their choices were sorely limited. She had to do her part.

Lucas reached for his cell lying on the table where his now-empty glass sat. She didn't have to ask to know the caller would be Simon making sure Lucas was aware of Victoria's appointment tomorrow morning.

The men in her life worked overtime to protect her. Rafe couldn't touch her. He could only play with her emotions. Clare and her partner, however, were a different story. Victoria wondered if Clare Barker was the entity of evil that Rafe insisted she was. Or was she a battered and neglected wife who had been used as a scapegoat by the most horrific of evils?

Victoria would know soon. Very soon.

Chapter Four

Olivia stared at the photos of her and her sisters as small children. She recognized the images of herself. Her adoptive parents had many photos taken during these same time frames, only Olivia was alone in those. She realized now, looking at this album, that none of the photos of her as a baby or small child back home had included her parents. Of course not. She had only come into their lives at age five.

But why were most memories before that time so completely lost to her? The average person remembered some part of their pre-school days. Olivia recalled very little. She had learned two weeks ago that her adoptive parents had worked hard to instill in her false memories that included them. She supposed that was why those years were so muddled. They had tried very hard to mesh her fully into their lives. To wipe away the ugliness of her early years.

The most disturbing part of this collection in front of her was the pictures from her life after the age of five. Several from each year. Every major event in her life was captured. Senior prom, high school graduation, college…everything.

"How is this possible?" Her head moved side to side as she stared at the captured moments to which whoever cre-

ated this album should not have had access. "Who did this?"
Her gaze connected with St. James's.

"You two ready to order yet?" The waitress who'd stopped
at their booth three times already paused once more.

Olivia blinked. She couldn't think of food right now. This
was…unsettling. Just when she thought the bizarre puzzle
couldn't get any more twisted, something new and totally
warped got thrown at her. Like this photo album of her life.

As the waitress hovered, St. James looked to Olivia.
"Something to drink at least?"

The impatience emanating from the waitress was hard to
ignore. "Water." Olivia exhaled a shaky breath. None of this
made sense. This part of her past was like watching some
sort of surreal reality series.

"Two waters." St. James offered the harried lady a smile
that was oddly distracting.

Olivia blinked again, tried to find her mental bearings.
Had her parents provided snapshots from her life as part of
the original adoption agreement? A question she intended
to add to her "need to know" list when she was speaking to
them again. Deep down she felt guilty for being on the outs
with the people who had raised and cared for her as their own.
They had been good parents. Still were. She loved them and
understood without reservation that they loved her.

"We aren't certain about that part," St. James said in answer to her question about how the more recent parts of the
photo album came to be. "But we do know that at the time
of the adoption each family was provided with photos of the
early years to allay questions later."

Questions from her…and her sisters. Olivia shook her head
again. "Why didn't they tell me?" She was an only child—at
least she'd thought she was. She and her parents had always
been so close. How could they have kept this from her as if
the information was irrelevant?

"That was a condition of the adoption. The secret was to be kept at all costs by all parties involved. Your parents were merely fulfilling their obligation to the legal contract they signed twenty-two years ago."

He made it sound so rational, so reasonable. As a paralegal, Olivia knew all about contracts. But this was morally wrong on so many levels. So, so many levels.

"Is your agency investigating Rafe Barker's claims of innocence?" Rafe's roundabout way of suggesting he was innocent had startled her. It shouldn't have. Most prison inmates would claim innocence, whatever their crimes. The fact that she was alive, as were her two sisters, lent credence to his claim to a degree that could not be ignored.

St. James considered her question for a moment. His pause made her want to squirm. Was there more she didn't know? She held his gaze, refusing to back off. Not an easy task. The man had amazing blue eyes, penetrating, hypnotic. He actually looked nothing like her idea of a private investigator. Thick blondish-brown hair that hugged the collar of his shirt. He dressed like the quintessential cowboy: well-fitted jeans, button-down cotton shirt, boots and hat. As handsome as he was, nothing about his appearance suggested skill as an investigator. He looked more like a celebrity cowboy— too well dressed and handsome to be a slave to a ranch or anything else. Didn't help that his voice was whiskey smooth and dark water deep.

Way off subject, Liv. Focus.

"We are looking into his claims," he finally said as if he'd waited for her to complete her mental inventory of his physical assets before interrupting.

Was that it? "Have you reached any conclusions?" Did she need to draw him a map to what she wanted? Why was it that everyone around her at the moment seemed determined to protect her by holding back? She was a big girl and the sooner he understood that the better. This was a pivotal moment in her life. There was so much she needed to know. And no one was cooperating.

"Mr. Barker claims he had nothing to do with any of the murders," St. James went on. "I don't have to spell out the ramifications of what that could mean."

That part she knew. Was everyone two decades behind the curve on this case? "Does your agency have reason to believe his claims have any merit? Is that why you took his case?"

Another of those pauses. "We didn't exactly take his case. His suggestion that you and your sisters are in danger prompted the head of the Colby Agency to take action to ensure your safety. That is our primary objective."

Olivia felt taken aback. "Does your agency make it a habit of taking up causes that don't feed the bottom line?" She had thought that perhaps notoriety was the motive. If the Colby Agency proved Rafe Barker's innocence in the eleventh hour, priceless publicity would be the payoff. Of course, there would be some unpleasant aspects to such a move but if true justice prevailed, the acclaim would be incredible.

The change in his eyes was unmistakable. Her suggestion that the agency might have a motive beyond doing the right thing didn't sit so well. Maybe she had grown accustomed enough to the dog-eat-dog world of the criminal justice system that her skin was thicker than most. Clearly his was not.

"We made a decision based on protecting lives," he informed her with a tone that broadcast loudly that her assumption had been correct. He was offended. "Rafe Barker made a decision about his future, but Clare is another story. If she's guilty then she represents a threat to you, your sisters and society."

"You have proof that she's committed any crimes?" As best Olivia could determine, there was every reason to believe the man with whom Clare was traveling was the guilty party in the criminal events since her release.

St. James shook his head. "None specifically. In fact, when Laney Seagers got her son back during the showdown at the old Barker home place in Granger, she felt certain that Clare helped the boy find his way back to her through the woods. Weeden appeared to be the one determined to inflict harm on anyone who got in his way of escaping."

Olivia frowned as she stared at the photos of Clare, her biological mother, posing with her three little girls. "But she's the one who only recently walked out of a maximum security prison. Weeden's history as a nurse would seem to indicate he's the selfless one." The scenario didn't fit…unless there were hidden secrets related to Tony Weeden she didn't know about. About any of the people involved, for that matter.

No question there. With the exception of fourteen days less leave time in her vacation account, she had nothing to show for two weeks' work on this case. Apparently neither did the Colby Agency.

"Beyond being a nurse and having had access to Rafe, who is this Tony Weeden?"

"We're still working on confirming certain details of his background," St. James said, his tone careful, his words well chosen. "We believe there's a connection between him and Clare beyond the obvious, but that scenario hasn't been confirmed."

In other words, she wasn't getting an answer. Until the news hit this weekend, Olivia had never heard the guy's name. According to St. James, Weeden was the one to smuggle the initial letter from Rafe to the Colby Agency. That was basically all she knew.

The waitress arrived with two glasses of ice water. St. James gifted her with another of those dazzling smiles and ordered a couple of burgers. Olivia wasn't sure she could eat but it was well past lunchtime and she recognized she needed to try. The mass of emotions and confusion just kept twisting tighter and tighter in her belly.

She didn't know how to feel about the Barkers. Her legal training warned that where there was this much smoke there was fire. Olivia had no reason to trust anything Rafe said… no reason to believe Clare was innocent based on her recent release or her actions since. The police had been no real help. The case was closed and they wanted to keep it that way. Unless Olivia could offer information on the missing bodies, they didn't want to hear what she had to say. To them, her digging screamed of reopening the case and trying to clear Rafe Barker of multiple homicides, and no one wanted any part of it. The community of Granger was already unsettled over Clare's release. Any suggestion of Rafe Barker's innocence was too much to tolerate.

Olivia had had no reason to consider trying to prove his innocence…at least not until now. He claimed he hadn't killed anyone and that his only responsibility was his ignorance of Clare's heinous deeds. Olivia was alive, her sisters were alive…did that mean he was telling the truth? Clare hadn't contacted anyone about protecting her daughters. She had taken several steps indicative of past or present criminal activity. Conversely, according to St. James, she had helped Laney Seagers find her son. Her activities since her release continued to send mixed messages as to her intent, which might make sense if the steps had been orchestrated by Weeden. Did that alone suggest she was innocent?

Not in a court of law…but then the Texas Supreme Court had made the decision that she was innocent based on the fact that no evidence had actually pointed to her. Twenty-two years ago the need to ensure the culprits responsible for such horrific murders were identified and punished had hastened the police's efforts and guaranteed the case had been pushed through trial despite the lack of tangible evidence against her. Charge and convict them both and the real killer got his or her just desserts. Didn't matter if the other was innocent. Too many innocent young lives had been taken for anyone to feel compelled to extend mercy. Clare had spent her entire sentence seeking out lawyers to take her case to one appeals court or the other. After the last appeal was lost, it had taken six years for Clare to find a legal team with the ability to get the job done. The woman hadn't given up.

Her tenaciousness reminded Olivia far too much of herself.

"Surely you can see our dilemma," St. James proposed. "No one wants an innocent man to be executed. Yet, we have no evidence that he is innocent. What we do know without doubt is that you and your sisters are at risk. As I said, our primary objective is to ensure your safety."

The circumstances cleared completely for her then. Raymond Rafe Barker had seventeen days to live and no one—*no one*—was focused on determining if he was guilty as convicted. There was only one thing Olivia could do.

The right thing.

"Has your agency explored the possibility of petitioning for a stay of execution until these questions can be answered?" It wasn't until just this moment that she grasped the concept that time was really slipping away. That he was her biological father was irrelevant in all this. Truth and justice were the only pertinent elements and no one appeared to be focused on those points. Not even the prestigious Colby Agency.

"The state district attorney is not prepared to take that step at this time. If we can bring him evidence beyond Barker's word he will entertain the possibility then and only then."

Indignation ripped through the more fragile emotions she'd been experiencing for days. "You have no evidence that he's innocent, that's true, but you do have new compelling evidence that the investigation twenty-two years ago was mishandled to some degree. That alone would likely persuade the governor to stay his execution pending further investigation."

St. James knew exactly what she was talking about. His expression closed her out as tightly as an isolated witness. "Mr. Barker specifically asked that your existence not be made public knowledge for your own safety."

Did he understand what he was saying? "Do you know the odds of getting a last-minute stay? These things take time and that's something we have very little of." Dammit. Did no one care if he was innocent or not?

"Typically we attempt to work within the client's wishes."

"Client? So you admit that he is a client?" Olivia reined in the cross-examination instincts. She held up her hands and waved them side-to-side as if she could erase the question. "Whatever your agency considers him, I would think that at the very least you have an obligation to bring this new evidence to the D.A.'s attention immediately."

His expression still closed, St. James eyed her cautiously. "We've already done that and he has chosen to wait it out and see what we find. Until we have something compelling he's not budging on his position."

"Unbelievable."

The burgers were delivered then but there was no way Olivia could eat. She clamped her mouth shut until the waitress had gotten another smile from St. James and scurried away.

Olivia pressed the issue. "He's aware that three of the murders charged against Barker were bogus and he wants to wait this out?" Incredible. It was men like that who had prompted her to go to law school to make a difference.

And that went well, didn't it, Liv?

"We have a whole team working on this, Ms. Westfield. We will find the truth."

"You are investigating his claims, then?" Why dance

around the admission. A whole team was working on the case and this guy wasn't owning up to what that meant?

"There was never a choice in the matter."

Ah, a man with an honorable spirit. He was either a former cop or soldier. Definitely not from her side of the law. "In my experience, Mr. St. James, good intentions are not always enough. Steps have to be taken now." Two calls were all she needed to make. She'd laid the preliminary groundwork already, even before she had any idea how this would shake down. Two simple phone calls would set the necessary actions in motion.

"If you submit the petition," St. James reminded her unnecessarily, "it becomes a matter of public record. How long do you think it will be before the press splashes your name as well as your sisters' across every headline in the state if not the country?"

Olivia ignored a prick of guilt. "Clare and Weeden have already made the news. It's only a matter of time before some ambitious reporter follows Clare's trail to us—if finding her daughters is her goal. This secret won't keep, Mr. St. James."

"I can see that you're concerned as to whether or not we can find the truth in time, which is completely understandable," he offered. "If you're open to suggestions, we could work together toward that end."

A frown tugged at her brow. What was he proposing? Wait, she got it. "Forming an alliance would provide you with the opportunity to keep an eye on me, is that it?"

He inclined his head and gave her one of those smiles he'd been flashing for the waitress. "That would square away both our quandaries as we move forward toward the same goal."

For the first time in a really long time, some random female chromosome that had gone into hibernation too long ago to remember abruptly hummed to life. That he had managed to resurrect such long-buried sensations startled her.

"You won't get in my way?" She knew what she had to do and she needed to be sure this man and his celebrated agency wouldn't try to stop her when they learned her intentions.

She was about to stir up a hornet's nest and no one, not even the Colby Agency, was going to like her methods. But Olivia was no fool. She could use all the help she could get. The Colby Agency likely had valuable connections that could serve her purposes. And she could use a team on her side.

"I will only get in your way if it's necessary to save your life. I presume you can understand that condition."

Another of those unexpected shimmers of attraction sizzled through her. "You've been watching me twenty-four/seven?"

"I have."

She'd suspected someone was following her. But day and night? "Is that the schedule you plan to keep?"

"Until Weeden is contained and we understand Clare Barker's intentions, that's the plan."

"You'll share your agency's findings?" That was key if he expected her cooperation.

"As long as you share yours." He draped a paper napkin across his lap, grabbed his burger with both hands and bit off a chunk of beef embellished with bun and fixings.

Olivia watched as he licked his lips and savored the explosion on his taste buds. Her stomach reminded her that she hadn't eaten since grabbing a two-day-old doughnut in the shabby motel lobby that morning. She chewed her lower lip and tried to recall the last time she'd enjoyed watching a man eat. Never came to mind.

He downed half the glass of water, and this, too, mesmerized her. The way the muscles of his throat worked and his fingers curled around the glass as it settled on the table once more. He licked his lips and she suffered a little hitch in her respiration. *Back up, girl. Back way, way up.*

"We have a deal, then?" he asked.

"Absolutely." She moistened her lips and braced to watch him dig into the burger once more.

He hesitated, the sandwich halfway to his mouth. "You skipped lunch. You should eat."

Olivia gave herself a mental shake. He would know what she'd eaten and where. "Sure. Right." She grabbed her burger and managed a nibble. Gave her something to do besides stare at him.

He flagged the waitress down and ordered a couple of colas. Olivia told herself not to stare at his mouth as his lips spread into another wide smile but the feat was impossible. That smile was fascinating. She worked with men in suits every day. Handsome, sophisticated men. Dressed in elegant attire. Men who lived in mansions and drove foreign sports cars that cost five times her annual salary. Not once had a single one ever muddled her ability to concentrate this way. She held her own with their impressive law degrees and their enormous egos. The few with the courage to make a pass or toss out a pickup line never made the same mistake twice.

This guy swaggers up to her in his tight jeans and well-worn boots and she turns to jelly? Had to be the emotional turmoil of the past two weeks. She wasn't herself. Ha! Of course she wasn't. She had just learned her entire history was made-up. She wasn't the daughter of Vincent and Nancy Westfield. She was the spawn of convicted serial murderers. Her biological father skated all around the idea that he was innocent while her mother flitted around setting fires and fleeing crime scenes. Evidently, any or all of those tainted genes she'd inherited were playing havoc with her logic and training.

The colas he had ordered arrived and he relished a long drink that once again fascinated her. "You have a plan of action in mind?" he asked.

Olivia swallowed at the lump the bite of burger had become, washed it down with water and cleared her throat. "The attorney I work with will file a petition for a stay of execution based on this new evidence." As she spoke she sent a text telling Nelson, her boss, to move ahead, focusing on the steps rather than the face of the man seated across from her. His eyes were a trap and she needed to avoid looking directly into those analyzing pools of blue. "Meanwhile, I'll start a press initiative in hopes of drawing out anyone who might know details not discovered twenty-two years ago."

"You hope to find information the police didn't find back then? It's been a long time, ma'am. People forget. You might come up empty-handed."

People did forget many things but few failed to recall murder. Especially in a small town like Granger. "Someone knows something. It's impossible that not one person in that small, close-knit community ever noticed anything peculiar about the two serial murderers living in their midst."

"Why wouldn't they have come forward before? It's doubtful that anyone wanted to see a murderer go free. Or an innocent man falsely accused. It goes against human nature."

"Maybe they were afraid or didn't realize the relevance of what they knew." She shrugged. "Or maybe they did come forward but the information was ignored or suppressed. Set aside for the greater good." Eight bodies had been exhumed from the Barker property. The police believed they had their killers. Why look anywhere else? The whole community if not the state had been screaming for justice.

"What if you don't find what you're looking for? Can you come to terms with that?" He pushed his plate aside, braced his forearms on the table and leaned toward her. "If some part of you is hoping this will have a happy ending—that maybe Rafe or Clare or both were falsely accused—you may be in for a major letdown, Ms. Westfield."

"Either way," she argued, "then I'll know, won't I?"

Chapter Five

Clare peeled away the tape that held the bandage on her son's arm. He'd instructed her on how to remove the bullet and suture the wound at their last stop. Her hands had been a little shaky but she'd gotten the job done.

"Have I told you how proud I am of you, son?" She smiled down at him. He was perched on the edge of the bed and had been very patient with her slow, arthritic hands.

He glanced at her and made a sound that was mostly a grunt. She imagined that praise was not something he'd received a lot of in his life. That, too, was her fault. She had made many mistakes in her time on this earth. Her decision to entrust to her evil sister the child born out of wedlock and as a result of a vicious rape was the first mistake. Janet had been born evil but like the devil himself she had returned to Clare's life after the death of their parents and presented herself as an angel of light. She wanted to help...to be friends.

How could Clare have been such a fool? And why hadn't that mistake made her smarter?

"You survived that evil witch and went on to become a nurse. That required hard work and much determination. That *is* an outstanding accomplishment." Particularly with one arm. That part she kept to herself.

Clare applied the antibiotic cream and clean bandages. There were things she needed to ask her son. Some more pressing than others. "Tony, did that awful man who took Lisa's little boy force you into killing him?" Her heart started to pound even as the words echoed in the cheap motel room. Their names and photos were all over the news. They were wanted as persons of interest in the murder of that terrible man who had taken little Buddy. This dump was the best they could hope for by way of a hiding place and still they would need to move soon.

"He was dead when I found him," Tony said, his words low, quiet, as always.

Clare's spirit lifted. "But the killer didn't harm the little boy. That's a blessing." Deep down that notion felt wrong to her. But she wanted to believe him.

"I think it was a drug deal gone bad. The boy was hunkered down in the backseat. The shooter might not have seen him. Probably saved his life."

That was a reasonable explanation. "I'm glad you were able to rescue him before anyone else got to him."

Silence settled around them as she taped the bandage into place. They were tired from running. Hungry. Stopping for food had been too risky. They'd had to hide the car Tony had bought in Brenham. They would retrieve it when it was time to move again.

"I checked with the hospital in Beaumont. Both that Mr. Camp and Mr. Hayden were released. I imagine that means they'll both recover from their injuries."

Her son grunted again. He hadn't meant to hurt either one of them. Over and over as she drove away from Granger and he huddled in the passenger seat he had assured her that he'd only been trying to protect her. She had been angry at what she had seen. Angry and fearful. She didn't want him to be like Janet…like Rafe.

His sincere insistence had calmed her. Sometimes extreme measures were necessary, she supposed. She had decided not to hold it against him. She was his mother; of course he would try and protect her the only way he had at his disposal.

"Have I told you how sorry I am that this happened?" She trailed her fingers along his right shoulder to the stub that was all that remained of his right arm. It pained her to think how he must have suffered losing a limb.

He turned to her, the gray eyes of his no-good father staring directly into hers. Thank God that cunning bastard had gone to hell just a few years after what he had done to Clare. A heart attack had been too good for him, but at least it had taken his rotten life and perhaps saved another young girl from such a travesty.

"I lied to you before," Tony admitted.

Clare had suspected as much. "You weren't injured in an accident when Janet was chopping wood?"

He shook his head. "I don't think you want to know the truth. It would be painful for you."

Clare blinked back the tears that burned her eyes. "Yes, I do." Her response was scarcely a whisper. Fear tingled up her spine. *Dear God, please don't let it be too horrible.*

"Janet sold me to the Weedens. They were old and didn't have any children of their own. They needed someone to do the work around their place and she needed money. Like always. Besides, she had her eye on an old man who had the money to give her the life she wanted. She didn't want me in the way."

Clare told herself to breathe but she couldn't draw the air into her lungs. She had learned the Weedens, both dead now, had been bad people. No friends. No connections in the community where they lived. Just plain old mean. Janet had relished in telling her that all those years ago…but Clare hadn't gotten the chance to do anything about it.

"When I was eighteen I tried to run away. They beat me. They always beat me and I never fought back. Not until that last time. I guess they knew they wouldn't be able to count on me after that. So they decided that if I wasn't going to be their workhorse I wouldn't be anyone else's, either."

"They did this to you?" Disbelief tinged her words.

"That day at lunch the old woman put something in my food. A sedative of some sort. It knocked me out." He stretched his back. "When I woke up they had me tied down and the old bastard had chopped off my arm with an ax."

The horror she had feared bloomed into a pain that cracked open her chest and ripped at her heart. "How did you survive?"

"I guess the old woman grew a conscience or worried they'd go to jail if I died. She tied a tourniquet around what was left of my arm and told me I'd better run. I got as far as town before I ended up in the hospital. Once I was recovered enough, I left the hospital and made a new life." He shrugged his uninjured shoulder. "End of story."

The weight of the decisions she had made back in college settled more heavily onto her shoulders. "I'm so sorry. This should never have happened to you."

He looked away. "You were raped. That shouldn't have happened to you. You did what you thought was right at the time. Janet took advantage of you. She took advantage of all of us."

Clare had done what she thought was right but she had been young and emotionally damaged. Otherwise she might not have made two mistakes so close together. "You did well for yourself in spite of my failure on your behalf." The terrible tragedy he had suffered was as much Janet's fault as hers. That brought Clare to yet another question she needed to ask. "How did you discover the truth about who you were? Did Janet seek you out?"

He shook his head. "It was easy enough."

When Janet had come back into Clare's life twenty-three years ago, Clare had asked her about her son and Janet had insisted he'd been adopted by a fine family who adored him. Lies, all of it. She had ruined Tony and then she'd shown up again to ruin Clare's husband and daughters. Janet'd had no one, evidently whatever man she'd gotten her claws into had either died or dumped her. Never one to go for long without someone to take advantage of, she had taken everything from Clare. Just before the arrests Janet disappeared but not before telling Clare that one day she would know how much her son had suffered with that *fine* family. Clare had had two decades to think about that…to think about all of it and to worry if her daughters were dead or alive.

Her hands shook with the fury that roared through her. Clare was glad her sister was dead. She hoped Janet Tolliver was burning in hell right this minute.

Clare cleaned up the mess she had made and turned to her son. "I'm going out to get us some food."

He tensed visibly. "That's not a good idea."

"It's safer for me than for you," she insisted. With his missing arm, he would be noticed by anyone he passed. She still had a chance of blending in, of being overlooked.

"I don't like it." He stood. "We'll go together."

Clare had to stand her ground here. Things had gotten out of control and she needed to try and regain some kind of order. Her quest was far too important to make any more mistakes, especially any involving the law.

She could not fail.

"Stay here, Tony," she said more firmly. "I will bring back supplies. Stay in the room."

He stood there for a moment that felt like an hour. "You won't leave me this time?"

Lord have mercy. She put her arms around him and held

him tight. The tears streamed from her eyes and she had no hope of stopping them. "I am so sorry I left you before. I swear I will never leave you again."

His arm settled around her in a loose hug. "All right, then. I'll be waiting."

Clare drew back and swiped her eyes. "Never doubt me again, son." She gave him her best smile. "I won't let you down."

Chapter Six

6:00 p.m.

In the Livingston café, Russ listened closely as Olivia made an appointment for eight this evening with a *Houston News* reporter. This television reporter, Keisha Landers, had earned first choice at an exclusive by virtue of being the daughter of the only reporter who had dogged every step the cops made during the Princess Killer investigation more than twenty years ago. Keisha's father, now deceased, had left all his notes with his daughter. Keisha had promised to share those with Olivia if she got an exclusive.

As relieved as Russ felt that Olivia had agreed to cooperate with his protection efforts, breaking the news about the Barker children being alive and well would likely turn this case into a circus. He'd warned her about that, but she insisted her way was the only way to prompt reactions in a timely manner.

He hoped she understood that the reactions she elicited might not be what she'd bargained for. Since there was no changing the lady's mind he had no alternative but to go with the flow. Making sure she stayed safe was his job.

They would both know soon enough. He had sent Simon a text warning him that the storm was about to hit. By noon tomorrow the petition for a stay of execution would be national news. The first interview of one of the Barker daughters, long thought to be dead and buried, would be hot on the same track.

"I'm meeting Keisha Landers and her cameraman at eight," Olivia informed him when she closed her phone. "I won't mention your agency. If she has questions about your presence, you're my personal security."

"This is your show." Whatever she thought, this was never going to go as smoothly as she hoped. The Colby Agency had already approached Landers about her father's notes. Anyone involved or closely associated with the original investigation had been contacted. Landers had suggested she intended to write a book about her father's documented journey following the case and she was not interested in sharing information. Russ couldn't imagine that her game plan had changed that much. The opportunity to capitalize was too appealing.

Olivia stood and picked up her bag. "I'd like to contact Sadie and Laney to see if they're interested in being a part of this. I assume you can assist me with that."

Russ slid from the booth and grabbed his hat before tossing a couple of bills on the table. "I'm waiting for word back from my superior. He notified the investigators providing protection to your sisters. I'll have a decision for you soon."

Olivia stared at him for a moment, those deep brown eyes searching his. "You don't trust me at all, do you?"

He was surprised to see regret in her eyes. They'd come a long way over burgers and colas. Her eyes gave him a peek beyond the tough-lady exterior she wore so proudly. "I want to trust you," he confessed. "I know your intentions are good. That said, I will admit that your take-the-bull-by-the-horns attitude is risky from my perspective."

"It's the only way."

Apparently done with talking, she did a one-eighty and headed for the exit. Russ followed. He'd given Simon a heads-up; there was little else he could do to waylay this collision course. Trying to keep the fallout minimal was the best he could hope for.

The bell over the café door jingled as he opened it for her to exit. The parking lot had been jam-packed when they arrived, forcing them to park on opposite sides. The trip to Houston would take no more than ninety minutes. Sufficient time for Simon to brace Sadie and Laney for the news that their older sister was going public.

"We could always leave your sedan at the motel," Russ suggested. "I'm happy to assume the role of chauffeur, as well." He sweetened the offer with a smile. Not that he was afraid of her giving him the slip, but it would allow him to stay abreast of any phone conversations. He hadn't had the opportunity to leave a listening device inside her sedan. Not to mention that sharing close confines with her wouldn't be a hardship. It would give him a chance to get a better handle on the lady. He'd been watching her for days on end. There was a lot he already liked about her.

She shrugged. "Works for me. That'll give me a chance to go over my own notes before the meeting."

Surprised that arm-twisting or further negotiations hadn't been necessary, he settled his Stetson in place and gave her a nod. "I'll follow you to the motel."

"Once we're on the road to Houston you can explain these unconfirmed details about Tony Weeden" She fished the keys from her bag. "I don't want to be hit with any surprises from Landers. Especially if it's information you already know."

Sensitive territory for sure. The way she looked at him warned she suspected he knew a lot more than he was sharing. "As long as you bear in mind that what we have so far is to a large degree speculation and that it's all off the record."

"I know. I know. I won't say a word to Landers." She

turned in the direction of her sedan. "You can trust me on that."

An explosion thundered in the air, and the ground shook with the blast that sent Olivia hurtling backward into Russ. His arms went around her as they were thrown to the ground. He rolled on top of her and shielded her body as debris showered onto the ground.

"You okay?" he demanded. Her face was pale. Her lips were moving, but he couldn't hear a damned thing she said. Instead of trying to make out her words he checked her body. No blood. No obvious injury.

He scrambled to his feet and checked the parking lot. Remnants of her tan sedan were scattered. The vehicles that had been parked on either side of it were damaged; one lay on its side. Thank God the lot had been empty of people save for the two of them.

The sound of screams and shouting echoed around him as patrons flooded out of the diner. He reached down and pulled Olivia to her feet. She stared at the mangled parts that used to be her sedan and then at him. For the first time since they'd officially met she was speechless.

"You two okay?" asked a tall, thin man wearing a white shirt sporting a name tag that identified him as Larry. He surveyed the parking lot and shook his head. "Oh, my God."

His ears were still ringing but at least Russ could distinguish the words being spoken now. He looked to Olivia and she gave a vague nod. Russ shifted his attention back to the man who had asked. "We're okay. Just a little shook up."

"I'm the manager," Larry explained. "I've got nine-one-one on the line and they're asking if we need medical assistance."

Russ turned back to Olivia. "You sure you're okay?"

She dusted off her skirt, her hands shaking. "The only

thing I need is a new car." She stared at what used to be her car, her expression a little shocky.

"We're good," Russ assured the manager.

From in front of the café door, a kid broke loose from his mother's tight grip and made a dash for Russ's Stetson. While the mother chased after her son, the manager inquired, "That your car?"

"Mine," Olivia answered. Using both hands, she reached up and tucked the hair behind her ears. She was steadier now but her face remained pale. She grabbed her purse and clutched it close as if she feared it, too, might be taken from her.

Russ surveyed the crowd around the diner entrance. "Might be a good idea to keep these folks inside," Russ suggested, "until the police determine there's no other danger." The property was bordered by businesses on either side but there didn't appear to be any damage beyond Olivia's car and the others parked nearest it. Like the diner's patrons, people had poured out of the other stores.

Larry's eyes widened as he realized the implications of Russ's words. "Come on, folks. Let's get back inside." After the promise of free dinner coupons for their next visit, the patrons filed back inside.

"Here's your hat, mister." The kid who'd escaped his mother beamed up at Russ as he held out the Stetson.

"Thanks." Russ claimed his hat and gave the kid a nod of approval before his frazzled mother dragged him back inside.

Olivia started toward where her car had been parked. He snagged her by the arm. "Whoa, there. You should wait inside until the police check things out."

The pale face was gone now, replaced by the flush of anger. "Someone blew up my car!"

Sirens wailed in the distance, the sound a welcome respite. He didn't want her attempting to rummage through the remains of her car. "That's a fact, but until the police do their thing, there's nothing we can do to figure out who or why. It'd be best if you wait inside."

Her brow furrowed into a frown. "I'm not going anywhere. If you can wait out here, so can I."

Since one of them had to speak to the police, he opted not to argue with her. "Just let me do the talking." Otherwise they would be here all night.

She glared at him but didn't disagree. Mostly, he decided, because her cell phone rang and distracted her. Four police cruisers barreled into the parking lot and Russ waited to see who was in charge. A detective would likely be en route. Bomb squad, as well.

"Are you serious? When did this happen?"

As she spoke into the phone, Olivia's face went pale again. Apparently there was more bad news. He had a feeling that she was going to need to reschedule her appointment in Houston.

When she ended the call, she looked from the uniforms approaching to Russ. "My motel room burned. Like twenty minutes ago." She shook her head. "My luggage was in the room." She stared at the spot where her sedan had been parked. "My briefcase was in my car."

Someone was not happy with Olivia Westfield.

9:20 p.m.

THIS WAS UNBELIEVABLE!

Olivia watched as the last piece of her car was loaded onto the truck that would haul it to the county crime lab for further analysis. The bomb squad had determined there was no further danger and the diner's patrons had been allowed to leave. No one had seen or heard anything other than the explosion. The remains of a homemade explosives device had been found. Not a totally rudimentary device, but not state-of-the-art, either. The detonator had been remotely controlled, which meant that whoever had set off the explosion had been watching and waiting for just the right moment.

She stood inside the diner and watched the final cleanup efforts. She had given the owners of the other two vehicles her insurance information. Whether or not her automobile policy covered this kind of thing, she had no idea.

"Would you like some more coffee, Ms. Westfield, before I shut down the coffeemaker?"

She glanced at the manager who had toiled away behind the counter for the past two hours. He'd served coffee and pie to the restless diners and to the policemen. Olivia imagined he was anxious to close up for the night. Thanks to her it had been a long one.

"No, thank you." She forced a smile on her lips. "I appreciate your patience and hospitality."

"No trouble, ma'am," he assured her. "I'm just grateful no one was hurt."

"Me, too." Whoever had done this had tried to get to her. If anyone had gotten hurt…

Was she doing the right thing going after this case, her past, with such a vengeance?

Olivia turned back to the scene transpiring beneath the parking lot lights before her lips started that telltale tremble and gave her away. She was so glad no one had been hurt. This was her fault. That part she understood completely, though no one had said as much. But she had seen the way the detective in charge had looked at her when she'd told him the only reason anyone would want to do such a thing was because of her looking into the Princess Killer case.

No one wanted her digging up that ugly past. Not even the cops, and they should want justice every bit as much as she did. She hugged herself and silently repeated the mantra that had gotten her this far. *It was the right thing to do.*

But was it?

St. James had gotten three calls from the Colby Agency following up on this development. He didn't say as much but she understood that no one was happy with her decisions. Olivia closed a hand over her mouth and stifled the urge to sob. Dammit, she was right to do this.

This had to be done. And there was no one else. Whoever had murdered those poor girls, whether Rafe or Clare or both, the world needed to know for sure once and for all. *She* needed to know. His eyes and that face…she closed her eyes and tried to put his image out of her mind. He just kept haunting her. Not one specific detail was familiar to her and yet there was a vague recognition of some sort. A knowing. Maybe it was more the sound of his voice. The voices from her dreams kept trying to surface.

Was she remembering ugly events from that terrifying time? She wanted to try to remember more…but the idea flat-out terrified her. She hadn't told a soul how much she feared those repressed memories.

She knew what they were. A visit to a shrink when she turned twenty-five and a particularly chilling dream had given her an answer. Whatever happened when she was a kid—and it was no movie—had been a true nightmare.

If Clare Barker had any motherly instincts at all she would have come to her daughters immediately upon her release and tried to set things to rights. She would have explained what the voices and the images meant. Was Olivia the only one who remembered? As the youngest, Sadie probably didn't remember anything from that time. But Laney was only a year younger than Olivia. Would she remember those awful sounds? The darkness? And those creepy feelings of terror?

Maybe she should meet with her sisters before she moved

forward with the meeting with Keisha Landers. The reporter was so anxious she had agreed to meet Olivia at whatever time she and St. James could get there—no matter the hour. Olivia sensed there was something the reporter felt needed to be discussed face-to-face. With all that had happened today, Olivia had to admit, even if only to herself, that she was a little anxious about all this, too.

St. James and the detective were talking again. She really should go out there and see if there was anything new. Mainly she just wanted this to be over. But they couldn't leave until the detective-in-charge gave the word.

What if the person responsible for the bombing had wanted to kill her? Would this quest she had set out to accomplish, no matter how much it hurt her adoptive parents, really be worth the steep price? Good grief, she should call them before they heard about any of this on the news.

She stared at her cell phone and tried to work up the nerve. Not happening. She told herself she needed to conserve battery power until she got another phone charger—since hers had gone up in smoke with the motel room. Later, when she'd picked up a few necessities, had her meeting with Landers and settled into a nice hotel in Houston, she would call home.

Except then it would really be late and her parents would be in bed. Maybe in the morning. Her name wouldn't be connected to anything before then. No reason to be hasty in making that call. They'd only worry more.

"Looks like they're wrapping things up."

Olivia started. She pressed her hand to her throat and felt instantly contrite. Larry, the diner manager, had moved up beside her at the window. "I'm sorry. I'm holding you up." She turned to him and extended her hand. "Thank you very much for being so kind through all this. I'm genuinely sorry for the trouble."

He gave her hand a shake. "You be safe, Ms. Westfield. Looks as if you have some bad people out to get you."

He had no idea. And she doubted he would be at all concerned with her safety once he learned who she was and what she was attempting to accomplish. She thanked him again and headed out to the parking lot to join her new partner.

Speaking of partners, Nelson had called. Everyone at the firm back home was worried sick about her. He would file the petition first thing in the morning. It had been too late to get it done today by the time she'd sent him the go-ahead.

St. James met her gaze as she moved closer, then he flashed her one of those killer smiles. Her heart skipped a beat. She told herself it was all the excitement and the emotional turmoil but she wasn't so sure.

"The detective says we're free to go," he told her in the deep voice that sent goose bumps tumbling over her skin. "As soon as they have anything on the forensics they'll let us know. I wouldn't count on anything that'll tell us who did this, but you never know."

Unless the forensics could tell her who had done this and put that person behind bars, anything else learned would be pointless to her. Her car was dead. Thankfully no one was hurt. Not much else mattered. She really would, however, like to know who wanted to stop her that badly.

"At least we can be in Houston before midnight." The possibility that Landers had information that would be useful to her investigation had Olivia ready to get on the road.

"The bomb squad checked my SUV," St. James told her as he gestured for her to precede him in that direction, "just in case. It's clean as far as explosives go. Other than the unavoidable signs of twenty-four/seven surveillance, I'm sure you'll find it an acceptable ride." As he opened the passenger-side door he flashed her another of those smiles that possessed the power to make her hormones sit up and take notice even at a time like this.

He hastily moved a battery-powered shaver and a bottle of aftershave from the front passenger seat. Tossed them into the backseat between a bag, probably carrying his clothes, and a backpack. An empty foam coffee cup and a half-empty bottle of water waited in the cup holders. The interior smelled of coffee and whatever aftershave was in that bottle and on his handsome face. The SUV was nice. Comfortable. Like him.

Olivia had no idea how exhausted she was until she fastened her seat belt and reclined in the leather seat. He was right. This would be a very acceptable ride. Maybe the bomber had done her a favor. Now she no longer had an excuse to avoid buying a new car.

Once they were on the highway, he interrupted the silence. "I'd like you to compile a list of the names of anyone you've spoken to about Rafe and Clare Barker and their case."

"You believe someone I've spoken to is responsible for destroying my car?" She figured as much herself. "Trying to scare me off?"

"That's exactly what I believe. The sooner we narrow down the possibilities, the more likely we are to head off another attempt at discouraging you."

"Besides you," she said pointedly, "there's my boss, Nelson Belden, the reporter we're going to meet, the detectives who investigated the case in Granger twenty-two years ago and about half a dozen former friends and neighbors of the Barkers. In my opinion," she said as she snuggled more deeply into the soft leather, "we should start with the minister of the small church they—we—attended. He was a little strange. There was one lady who used to help out with the animals from time to time at the vet clinic the Barkers operated in that barn on their property. She actually threw rocks at me as I ran back to my car after asking my first question at her door."

He laughed. The deep rumble seemed to close around her in the darkness, made her feel warm and safe. *Silly, Liv. So very silly. You don't even know this man.*

"She actually threw rocks at you?"

"Yes. She chased me off the porch and as I ran across the yard, she threw those white stones she'd used as a sort of mulch in her flower bed."

Another deep chuckle. "We'll definitely put her on the list. Right under the investigating detectives."

If he hadn't said the last so soberly she might have thought he was kidding. "You want to start with the cops?"

"If a mistake was made in the investigation, they have the most to lose."

Neither she nor he laughed this time.

Chapter Seven

Houston News, 11:55 p.m.

Keisha Landers wasn't exactly happy to have a third party present during the interview. Russ wasn't surprised by her reaction, but Olivia convinced the lady to permit him to stay. Thankfully Olivia hadn't mentioned the name of his employer, which was good since he knew the agency had contacted Landers to no avail. If the television reporter had something significant to bring to the table, they would know soon enough. If her anxious demeanor was any indication, this could be the break Olivia and her sisters needed. The one that could solve this puzzle, finally.

Twenty-two years was a long time for anyone to wait. Even if they hadn't known they were waiting for this moment until very recently.

The *Houston News* conference room wasn't as large as the one at the Colby Agency but it was big enough for staff meetings and morning briefings. Olivia sat next to him, the reporter seated on the other side of her. Coffee had been brewed and all three had a fresh, steaming cup. Russ suspected they would need a second before the meeting concluded. Mostly he was thankful Olivia hadn't put up a fuss when his boss made the decision that under the circumstances it was too dangerous to have the Barker girls meet. To Russ's surprise, Olivia had agreed for now. She would meet her sisters at a later time.

Landers had sent her cameraman home after he set up the camera. She had decided this interview needed complete secrecy. Now, as they got started, she sat a box of material on the table. A standard-size cardboard file box the average person used for storing papers and receipts from the previous year. The once white box was yellowed with age and the corner creases weren't so sharp anymore. The reporter removed the lid and set it aside.

"After Clare's release," Landers began, "I recalled my father working endlessly on the case." She smiled sadly. "I was just a kid and every night during the investigation and then the trial I would ask my mother when my dad was coming home. She would always say that he was trying to help the missing princesses." Her expression grew distant. "I didn't understand what she meant at the time, but later, after his funeral, she mentioned that he always regretted not being able to do enough on that one."

"Your father was a newspaper man his whole life?" Olivia asked.

Landers nodded. "He started out as a delivery boy at the age of ten and came home with ink on his hands until the day he died." Her smile brightened. "He insisted that a good reporter was only as good as his next story. Didn't matter how great the last one was, it was the next one that defined you."

Russ sipped his coffee and analyzed the woman's voice. It was thick with emotion. There was something big in that box. Her anticipation was as palpable as her respect and fondness for her father's memory.

Landers removed bundle after bundle of photos and notes from the box. She unwrapped each, one by one, then began to pass them to Olivia. "The story was never going to be a routine homicide piece." She laughed dryly. "Not that there's ever anything routine about homicide. According to his notes, my father grew more and more disturbed by what he didn't find in the police reports."

"You have copies of the police reports?" Olivia asked, clearly surprised. "I asked to see the files and they turned me down flat. When my boss, Attorney Nelson Belden, followed up with a written request, he received a letter stating the case files had been misplaced."

"My father had friends," Landers explained. "One of his buddies in Houston P.D. got copies of everything for him." She passed the next bundle to Olivia. "Crime scene photos, lab results, interviews with friends, neighbors, anyone and everyone who was interviewed."

"This is incredible." Olivia moved the photos and papers closer to Russ so that they could study them together.

Some of the photos he would have preferred she not see. Blood on the sheets of the bed she and her sisters had shared. Blood in the closet and in the bathroom. A booking photo of Clare looking frazzled and wild-eyed with fear, or something along those lines. Rafe's booking photo with him appearing calm and composed. The stark difference had Russ taking a second, longer look. What kind of man looked so cool at a time like that?

More photos of the numerous digging expeditions in the woods on the Barker property. Olivia stared long and hard at the images of remains.

Finally, she moved on to the official scene investigators' reports and the interviews. They must have read for a half hour or more and were scarcely through half the neatly typed forms when Russ recognized what Landers's father had seen more than two decades ago.

Every single person who had known the Barkers described Clare as a quiet, obedient woman. She did exactly as her husband told her and never dared defy him. Several stated in no uncertain terms that Rafe ruled her and the children with an iron fist. The minister Olivia thought to be odd even said as much. Clare was kind and generous and quiet, he'd said. A good, obedient wife and loving mother.

The physical evidence all pointed to Rafe. The connection between the physical evidence and Clare was negligible to the point of being nearly nonexistent. Each detective concluded that the evidence was such that Clare couldn't possibly have been oblivious to the heinous deeds, thereby making her complicit.

Russ read copies of letters the victims had sent to Rafe thanking him for his wonderful work rescuing pets. The Barkers had been known far beyond the boundaries of their community for their animal rescue work. Veterinarians from many surrounding counties had sent folks there to view the many animals up for adoption. Grateful kids, most often young girls, sent letters thanking Rafe for their new pet. The letters were placed on a bulletin board, some accompanied by a photo of the girl and her pet. The bulletin board was labeled "the princesses." All the victims' photos were there, the ones found as well as the ones who remained unaccounted for. That was how the case had gotten its moniker.

"Do you see how it all points to Rafe until that final morning before the arrest?" Landers queried.

Olivia nodded. "The blood the police suspected came from my sisters and me was the only actual physical evidence that tied Clare to anything. And since we're all three alive, we know that was planted."

"The blood," Landers countered, "and the fact that several of the murdered girls were buried on the property."

"But that doesn't prove Clare helped murder or bury a single one," Olivia insisted. "There was no conclusive evidence that she was involved."

"The consensus," Russ felt compelled to add since the two

appeared at such odds on the issue of Clare's involvement, "was that Clare and Rafe worked as a team. It was difficult for most to accept that Clare had no idea what her husband was up to considering how close the two appeared to be. Where one was seen, the other was always nearby. That she was so submissive to him makes the idea far less acceptable, as well. In my opinion, her conviction was more about perception and possibility than evidence."

"Agreed," Landers said. "Those very elements, though not evidence themselves, speak to motive and opportunity. That conclusion, whether biased or not, and the blood confirmed to be you and your sisters' type were instrumental in Clare's conviction and, as we all know, in the overturning of that conviction. The evidence was circumstantial at best and the Texas Supreme Court recognized that reality."

Olivia lapsed into silence for an extended period. Russ wondered if it was more than she could absorb in one sitting.

"We should finish this tomorrow," he offered. "Today has been a hell of a ride and it's late."

Landers put her hands up in a show of no protest. "I do understand. We can start fresh in the morning."

For an ambitious reporter she was far more reasonable than he'd expected. Five or six years older than Olivia, she had followed in her father's footsteps only she'd chosen television over newspaper reporting, making quite the name for herself in Houston. It was obvious to Russ that this case had thrown her for an emotional loop, as well.

But no one was more emotionally slammed than Olivia and her sisters. This was a test of will for Olivia, but the waiting and not knowing had to be difficult for Sadie and Laney, too.

"If Clare wasn't involved," Olivia said, finally breaking her silence, "maybe there was someone else." The pitch of her voice rose with each word. "Someone who was right there all along that no one knew about."

Russ wondered where that had come from. Something she remembered or wishful thinking? Maybe Olivia just needed one of her biological parents to be a normal person.

"There's no mention of close family in any of the interviews," Landers pointed out. "No friends who visited. Just Rafe and Clare and their daughters. Do you remember anyone else frequenting the house or the clinic?"

Olivia considered the question for several seconds before shaking her head. "I barely remember anything. Mostly what I recall comes in the form of nightmares and none of it is clear. I just feel like there's something we're missing. Something or someone." She shook her head. "I don't know."

"Have you ever considered regression therapy?" Landers asked her.

Russ had wondered the same thing. Olivia had been old enough to have more substantial memories than her younger sisters. But regression therapy was not for the faint of heart. And sometimes there was nothing gained.

"I never had any reason to consider it until now." Olivia stared at the mound of documentation. "The only people who know the whole truth are Rafe and Clare. He's either lying or she's keeping a secret that could have cleared her during the trial."

Olivia was right on both counts. "If anyone else was involved, Clare would have known that person," Russ said, voicing what Olivia hadn't. "She and Rafe were together all the time." He gestured to the documentation on the table. "Wherever those interviewed saw one, they saw the other. But if Rafe pulled disappearing acts to assuage his dark urges or went off with some other person to do the same, why didn't Clare say as much at trial?"

The first person who came to his mind was Clare's sister, Janet Tolliver. Janet had arranged for the secret adoptions of the girls. She had kept the photo albums all those years.

And she'd taken care of Clare's son, Tony Weeden, they suspected, after Clare's rape in college. Why had she never been seen by any of the folks in Granger who knew the Barkers? Surely she had visited her sister at some point, unless they were estranged again by then. Either way, why hadn't Janet been at the trial?

And why the hell had she been murdered shortly after Clare's release from prison?

"Maybe Clare was protecting someone," Olivia offered. She turned to Russ. "But why do what she's been doing since her release? If she was wholly innocent, why behave guilty now? What's the point?"

"I think you need to ask her that." This from Landers.

"That could pose a risk to her safety." Russ made the statement a little more forcefully than he'd intended, but he didn't want Landers putting any ideas in Olivia's head. She was already plotting enough strategies that had garnered her the wrong kind of attention.

"Besides," Olivia mentioned, "it's doubtful that she would come forward at this point and chance being arrested."

"Basically," Landers summed up, "Clare Barker is in the same position now that she was in twenty-two years ago. Whatever she knows that would clear her name, she can't share because coming forward would pose an equally unwanted effect on her future as a free woman."

Russ suspected the reporter was far more correct than she knew. "We've completely ignored this newest development." When he had their attention, he went on. "Someone sent Olivia a very powerful message this evening. Frankly, it's doubtful that the bombing could have been carried out by Clare or Weeden. He was injured in the shootout in Granger this weekend and there is absolutely nothing in his background that indicates he has any explosives experience or that he has attempted to learn the basics via the internet. The police have gone over his home and computer. There's nothing that would suggest he had the skills or the inclination for a move like this."

"Doesn't mean he didn't use someone else's computer or a public access computer," Landers argued. "There are ways of getting information without the trail leading back to you."

"Bomb making can be tedious work," Russ countered, "and would be best accomplished with two hands." Tony Weeden only had one, which Russ didn't need to point out.

"Clare may have helped him," Olivia tossed out.

"Like she helped Rafe?" Russ was leaning toward the idea that Clare was a pawn in all this. Maybe not an innocent pawn, but a pawn nonetheless.

Olivia rubbed at her temples with her forefingers. "Maybe. I'm beginning to wonder if anyone in this nightmare could be innocent in the true sense of the word."

"Tony Weeden served as Rafe's nurse for several years," Landers said. "Is it possible he's following Rafe's orders to draw Clare back into a trap that will somehow frame her for something unthinkable all over again? Rafe only came forward after she was released. Unless you actually believe his motive in doing so is sincere."

Olivia laughed but the sound was far from amused. "I have no idea what his motive is. I can see the validity in your point in terms of his intentions toward Clare." Olivia turned to Russ once more. "Like ensuring she was charged with killing her daughters for real this time or at least attempting to. But why would he do that? Why not just have Weeden or someone else kill Clare if he wants revenge against her for some reason we can't see? Since we have no idea what the truth is, we have to consider that Rafe could be correct and that wanting her daughters out of the way is what Clare wanted all along. But why? What's her motive? How can we possibly hope to know one way or the other if we don't find Clare and persuade her to talk to us? We need more than Rafe's side of the story."

"Finding her might be within our power," Russ reminded her, "but we can't persuade her to tell us anything she doesn't want to share. And if Rafe is behind all of this, Clare may be as much a target as you and your sisters."

Landers picked up on his reasoning. "To go there, Mr. St. James, you would have to presume that she had been the one to hide her daughters away and that Rafe is now attempting to punish her since she got to go free and he didn't. You looked him in the eye today, Olivia. Do you believe the man you spoke to is capable of going to those extremes?"

Olivia shook her head. "I don't know. I was so taken aback by the reality that he was, in fact, my father that I can't trust any conclusions I formed."

Landers gathered several of the reports, tucked them into a folder and handed it to Olivia. "Start with the detectives who investigated the case. My father had another adage that he shared with my mother and me regularly. The one thing you could always count on in an investigation was that the cops would put on paper what they wanted you to know and nothing more. Whatever they left out is the part you need to find."

Olivia felt numb as she left the *Houston News*. It had been almost twelve hours since her meeting with Rafe Barker and she was more confused now than she had been when she walked out of that prison. Could she force the investigating detectives to discuss the case with her now that she had copies of their interviews? Or did she go straight to the sources and see if anything new came of her questioning, as she'd planned to do before meeting with Keisha Landers? Not that her first attempt had garnered her any information. But she had their signed statements now. That might make a difference.

She waited while St. James checked his vehicle for tampering. The sounds from the explosion kept haunting her.

That deafening boom, the screams…the falling debris. Her hearing had scarcely returned to some semblance of normal when they reached Houston. There was still a little ringing but she could hear fine. Had that explosion been intended to kill her? Had it gone off too early? No wait. That couldn't be right. St. James had said the explosive had been remote detonated, which meant whoever set it off had been watching her. If he'd wanted her dead she would be dead.

"You can get in now."

Olivia snapped from her worrisome thoughts. He'd already opened the passenger-side door and was waiting for her to move. "Thanks." She climbed into the seat and tried to go over what she'd learned tonight in a more logical manner, without all the emotions she'd suffered as she'd heard and read the information for the first time.

When he'd settled behind the wheel she made a decision, but she waited until he was out of the parking lot and rolling along the deserted street before making her announcement.

"I need to see my sisters." It was the only way. Between the three of them perhaps they could remember something relevant. Whether they did or not, Sadie and Laney needed to know what was going on and Olivia wanted to tell them face-to-face.

"We discussed that already. That would be a strategic error."

"I understand there's danger but they need to know about this. What on earth do you mean strategic error?" Was he talking about the danger? What? After all she'd been through today, she didn't want any more cryptic statements from him. She wanted straight answers. There was no reason for him to try and keep her from her sisters.

"The best way to keep the three of you safe is by keeping you apart. You said you understood that reasoning."

That made no sense to her now. None at all. "Explain how

that helps, if you don't mind. You said we had to find the truth. At this point, I can't see that happening without the three of us putting our heads together."

They were supposed to be cooperating. She had taken him into her meeting. She had convinced Landers to share what she had with him. Why wasn't he doing his part by rethinking this issue?

"If the ultimate goal is to take the three of you out," he said as he slowed for a turn, "having you together in one place makes the job a lot easier."

She wanted to rant at him but the truth was, he had a point with that one aspect of her request. "Whoever is following me would be led to the others—that's what you're saying. I get it."

"That's what I'm saying."

Dear God. Rafe Barker was in prison. Clare was God only knew where with her wounded accomplice. Who did that leave to put them in danger?

One or more of the detectives who had conducted the original investigation? A surviving family member of one of the victims? Who? There was absolutely no way to know.

And what about the theory that someone else was involved? Was that person still out there, praying the truth would not be discovered and out her or him?

"And if we run out of time without finding the answer?" Rafe Barker had just over two weeks to live.

"We won't," he said with complete certainty. "We will find the truth without putting you and the others in more danger."

St. James was right. There was no point arguing the issue. She couldn't go near her sisters until they knew the answer to who killed all those little girls. Since Rafe did nothing but speak in riddles, the only other real source was Clare. Whether she would tell the truth—if they found her—was anyone's guess.

"We should go to Granger and interview the people whose

statements Landers feels are the most telling as to how poorly the investigation was handled." Olivia would love another shot at the minister. And the lead detective, Marcus Whitt. If she couldn't meet with her sisters, she could at least do this.

"That we can do," St. James allowed. He glanced her way. "After some sleep."

She couldn't argue with that point, either. The exhaustion had gotten the better of her the past few minutes or the subject of a meeting with her sisters wouldn't have come up again. She wasn't thinking rationally. She needed sleep desperately. The only question would be whether or not her mind would shut down long enough for her to get any.

Her cell rang out and she fished through her bag to find it. Surely Nelson wouldn't still be up at this hour. Her chest cramped with the idea that it could be one of her parents. They wouldn't call this late unless something was wrong. If something had happened after the way she'd left things…

Fear had a choke hold on her by the time she found her phone and managed a greeting.

"Olivia, it's Keisha."

Olivia relaxed. "Is something wrong?" The reporter's voice sounded strained and uncertain.

"I was thinking," Keisha said, "that if you're going to Granger to do some follow-up interviews, I'd like to be a part of that. I believe this story deserves some patience. I'm willing to withhold running my story until we've investigated further. Would that be agreeable with you and your associate?"

They could use all the help they could get. "That would be most agreeable. We could meet for breakfast, discuss strategy and head for Granger. Say nine at the Broken Egg?"

Keisha agreed with the time and her choice of cafés and Olivia thanked her and ended the call.

"I assume that means we'll have company on our field trip?" St. James asked.

"She knows more about the investigation than either of us," Olivia countered, stating her case. "She's a valuable source. Involving her assures continued cooperation."

St. James gifted her with one of those knockout smiles of his. "Smart move."

Maybe they would make a good team, after all.

Chapter Eight

Russ checked the locks on the door one last time. Taking a room in the rear of this low-rent motel provided protection to some degree against being spotted from the street. He'd made sure they hadn't been followed from the television station but the situation remained less than optimal. Tomorrow Simon Ruhl would arrange for an alternate vehicle, since whoever had followed Olivia and placed the explosive beneath her sedan had no doubt seen Russ's SUV. He'd scanned his SUV for tracking devices and found nothing. Still, he would feel more secure when they had a different vehicle and a safe location to lay low. For now this would do.

He'd considered taking Olivia to his place, but tracking them there would be too simple for anyone who knew his name. That wouldn't take long if their tail had access to the right database for running license plates. As a former cop himself he didn't want to believe any of the detectives or officers involved with the investigation twenty-two years ago would go to these kinds of extremes to scare Olivia off but he couldn't dismiss the possibility. Particularly not after her less than hospitable experience in Granger.

Simon had someone checking into the four cops and the one FBI agent who had served as the primary investigators on the joint task force that worked the Princess Killer case. Most cops had some training when it came to explosives, but the type used on Olivia's car required a good deal more than a basic knowledge.

The bathroom door opened and Olivia peeked out. "You decent?"

She looked young and way too vulnerable in her pink pajamas. Her hair was still damp and her brown eyes looked wide with uncertainty. Definitely not the sharp, don't-get-in-my-way lady he'd met that morning. This was the unguarded Olivia. Weary with emotion. As tired as they both had been when they left the *Houston News,* they'd made a quick run through an all-night superstore for necessities she would need. A woman's idea of necessities was definitely different from a man's. Olivia had required two changes of clothes, pajamas, cosmetics and hair products. He, on the other hand, had selected one item—bottled water.

"It's late," he teased, "any decency I possess goes into hiding at midnight."

She scowled at him as she slipped from the tiny bathroom and padded to the first of the double beds. Her scrutiny quickly shifted to the bed as she peeled the covers back. "I hope they don't have bedbugs."

For a woman who had faced her biological father, the convicted serial murderer, and the total destruction of her car via a homemade bomb, worrying about bedbugs seemed a minor nuisance.

"I hear they never linger in the bathtubs if you'd prefer to sleep there."

She shot him another of those dark scowls. He laughed, couldn't help himself.

"It's not a laughing matter. Those things bite and if you take them home with you they're a big problem to get rid of."

"I would have been more worried about the last place you were staying." Compared to that one, this place was a resort.

"I checked their health department rating and the incident reports," she said as she surveyed the sheets. "No pests reported."

"You can check that?" He should have known the lady would be thorough in whatever she did.

"You can." She collapsed on the bed in a cross-legged position. "You don't do that when you travel?"

"This is my first overnight duty since before the bedbug issue got its own byline." He toed off his boots and stretched out on the other bed without bothering to check for critters.

"You're living dangerously, Mr. St. James," she warned with enough of a twinkle in those big brown eyes that he knew she was teasing. She didn't smile often but her eyes made up for it. She had gorgeous eyes. Wide, dark and infinitely inquisitive.

She frowned. "Actually, I suppose I'm the one living dangerously. It was my car that blew up."

"I was just about to point out that fact." He twisted his lips into a wry smile. "You haven't made any enemies at work, have you?" That was an area he hadn't explored. He doubted her life, beyond the fact that her biological parents were the Barkers, was at play here but asking seemed a logical step.

"None that I know about."

She leaned onto her side and propped herself up on the stack of pillows, stretching her long legs, which would have been a nice distraction had she not been wearing neck-to-ankle concealing flannel. Had it not been for that infernal clearance rack she would be wearing one of those gauzy thin summer nightshirts.

"You were going to tell me about the possible connection between Weeden and Clare your agency had discovered, but we got a little sidetracked."

"We found Clare's college roommate from her freshman year. She claims Clare was sexually assaulted by one of her professors and a pregnancy resulted. She had no proof and a birth was never documented. We're exploring the possibility that Tony Weeden was the result of that assault and maybe Clare gave him to her older sister to take care of, only her sister turned him over to a couple, the Weedens, who had no children."

"Janet Tolliver, the woman who was murdered," Olivia ventured, "is without question Clare's sister? And she orchestrated the adoptions of me and my sisters? That's confirmed?"

"We've confirmed that Janet was Clare's sister. There was an incident when Clare was very young and Janet was sent away to live with another family that eventually adopted her, the Tollivers. Hers and Clare's parents, the Sneads, were murdered several years later when Clare was eight years old. But that's as far as we've been able to substantiate our suspicions. The rest is as much speculation as anything." He sat up and reached for the stack of interview reports Landers had given them. "We're assuming that, since Janet had possession of the photo albums and Rafe named her as his co-conspirator, she was the one who took care of the adoptions, but we have no confirmation other than Rafe's word."

Olivia tucked her hair behind her ear and snuggled into her pillow. Her eyes had grown heavy but she wasn't ready to give up just yet. The need to know more was driving her even as tired as she obviously was. "Why was Janet sent away? Did the family have financial problems?"

That was a fair question. The agency had considered that possibility first since it wasn't unheard-of for a family to make a decision like that back in the day. But that wasn't the case. "When Clare was three years old, Janet tried to harm her. Evidently the incident was bad enough that the parents felt removing her from the home was necessary."

Olivia sat up. "What kind of people are we talking about here?" She pushed to her feet and started to pace. "Janet was my aunt by blood and she tried to harm her own baby sister. My parents are convicted murderers." She stopped and turned to stare at Russ. "My older half brother has probably murdered at least one person." The pacing resumed. "How could anyone in their right mind want to risk passing on those kinds of genes?"

"Some of what I just told you is speculation, some is hearsay. It may not be as bad as you think."

She paused again to glare at him. "Do you really believe that?" A frown tugged at her eyebrows. "Wait. You said Clare's parents—my grandparents—were murdered? How? Why?"

More questions she would regret asking. "When Clare was about eight years old someone came into the house and brutally murdered them...." Russ took a breath. "They used an ax. The killer was never found, but at least one eye witness reported seeing a young girl, a teenager, near the home at the time. Considering what we know about Janet, we think it might have been her exacting revenge for having been abandoned. Again, that's supposition on our part."

"Oh, my God." Olivia wilted back down onto the bed. "That explains the nightmares. I've had them my whole life and now I know why. My aunt was an ax murderer and my parents, one or both, are sociopaths, too."

Russ sat up, dropped his feet to the floor and rested his forearms on his thighs. "Tell me about your nightmares." She'd mentioned them in the meeting with the reporter. Anything she recalled could prove useful to the investigation. And maybe it would get her mind off genetics.

Olivia pulled her knees up to her chest and wrapped her arms around her flannel-clad legs. "They're mostly dark. Creepy. The typical childhood night terrors. My parents— my adoptive parents—always blamed some movie I watched with my cousin when I was five." She hesitated as if she'd just realized the timing. "Of course, they told me that since it was the easiest way to explain any memories that might have surfaced from my life before becoming a Westfield." Her eyes filled with pain. "When I confronted them they told me how bad it was that first year. I was practically catatonic. They held me out of school an extra year in hopes I would be better adjusted before thrusting me into a new stressful situation."

The thought of what she may have witnessed as a child twisted inside him. How could either of her parents have been truly innocent? How could either not have known what the other was doing?

"Do you remember anything at all from the nightmares? Images, sounds or voices?"

"I remember darkness. Always the darkness." She rested her head on her knees. Her voice had turned so low and quiet that he wondered if she was reliving those awful moments. "And the screaming. Lots of screaming."

"Was it you screaming? Or one of your sisters? Were the screams close to you or coming from someplace else? Another room maybe?"

"Not me." She frowned in concentration. "I mean, it wasn't my voice. But it wasn't another child's, either. I think it was an adult."

"A woman's screams or a man's?" Olivia might know far more than she realized, Russ thought. The slightest piece of information, like who was screaming, could make a difference.

"A woman's. Absolutely a woman's." Her expression told him that she was searching the past, seeking those vague nuances from her memory banks. "She wasn't in the room with us." She shrugged. "I guess it was a room but it was small, cramped and very dark. Pitch-black."

"Was there anyone in the room with you?" She had two

younger sisters; chances were they had been with their big sister.

She mulled over that question for a bit. "I think so. There was shaking and soft…" She inclined her head and appeared to concentrate hard. "There were softer sounds, like sobbing or whimpering but so soft I might be mistaken. Maybe it was just me breathing."

"When you wake up from the nightmares are you still in the dark room listening to the screams?"

She gave a slow, hesitant shake of her head. "I'm in a bigger room and there's blood. Everywhere." She shuddered. "I hear this humming. Some tune I should know but I don't. That's when I wake up. Screaming, usually."

She took a big breath. "I don't want to talk about this anymore tonight." Her lips curved into a forced smile. "Good night." She switched off the lamp on her side of the table between the beds and curled up with her pillow.

"G'night." Russ hadn't enjoyed pressing her on the issue but there was something there. If she'd seen blood in the house, then she may have witnessed one of the murders.

Sixteen days was all the time they had left before Rafe Barker would be executed. They needed a break in this investigation. A single scrap of information that would point them in the right direction.

After checking the lock on the door again and the rear parking lot via the window, he grabbed his bag and moved to the bathroom. Too damned tired to do more than strip off his clothes and leave them in a pile, he climbed into the shower and set the spray to hot. He left the door open. Closing it was too much of a risk. Privacy be damned.

The water immediately started to loosen up his stiff muscles. He'd been running on adrenaline for hours now. With a trip to Granger on the agenda in just a few hours, he needed at least a little sleep. Judging by what Olivia had encountered in Granger already, the welcome, particularly from the local authorities, would probably be less than friendly. He needed to be on his A game.

His shower took all of three minutes. He dragged on a clean pair of jeans and a tee, checked the parking lot again, tucked his weapon under his pillow and then collapsed into the bed.

With the bathroom light filtering from the crack where he'd left the door ajar, he watched Olivia sleep. Like her sisters, her life would be vastly different after all this. He hoped she would find the peace she needed to move on from here.

Nothing about it was going to be easy.

THE DARKNESS WAS THICK ENOUGH to touch. She could feel it vibrating around her. And the screams... Oh, the screams were so terrifying. She wanted to scream, too, but she kept her teeth clenched to hold back the fear bulging in her throat. Her heart rammed harder and harder against her breastbone.

Mommy...

Her mommy was screaming. And the crying, softly agonizing. Her sisters were crying and she couldn't help them. She did as she was told. She took them into the closet and they hid. Huddled together in that tiny space, their trembling bodies vibrating like an unbalanced washing machine on the spin cycle.

Bad things were happening and Olivia couldn't make them stop. She could hear the awful sounds. Wailing and screaming. There would be blood. There was always blood. So much blood.

The dogs were barking. She could hear them out in the clinic. They knew something was wrong, too. But they couldn't stop it, either. There was nothing to do but hide and hope the monster wouldn't get them. Mommy always said when the monster came they had to hide and be very, very quiet.

He was here tonight. And this time he might just get them all....

Waking with a start, Olivia bolted upright. The air sawed in and out of her throat even as it tried to close. The nightmare. Just another nightmare. She shouldn't have talked about it. That only made it worse...made it more vivid.

Arms reached around her in the darkness. She screamed and tried to pull away.

"Olivia, it's me, Russ."

The voice sounded familiar and strong. Light chased away the darkness and she saw his face. Russ St. James. The man Rafe Barker had sent to protect her.

Olivia hugged her arms around her knees and fought harder to stop the trembling. "Sorry. It was...the nightmare."

The same old nightmare, this time on steroids. She swiped at her face, only then realizing she had been crying. So much worse this time.

St. James scooted closer, settling on the bed beside her. "You're okay now."

"Of course I'm okay," she snapped. She wasn't a child. She didn't need him taking care of her. "I'm fine."

"Well, I wouldn't go that far." He chuckled softly. "That must've been a hell of a nightmare. If we had any neighbors someone would have called the police by now."

God. She pressed her forehead to her knees. "I'm sorry."

"There's no need to be sorry. You need some water or something?"

A good stiff drink would be more suitable. She lifted her head and sighed. "No. I'll pull it together in a minute."

She wanted to resent that he was so close. Hovering around her with his big strong body all warm and solid. But she couldn't. She actually wanted to lean into him and try to forget. But she couldn't forget. Anything she could remember might help solve this awful mystery.

"Do you feel up to talking about it?"

She dared to meet his gaze. The concern in those blue eyes almost undid her. She had to look away. "It was the same only this time I remember more. It's like you said, my sisters were there with me. In a closet. That's why it's so dark. We would hide in the closet whenever the trouble started. I can hear her screaming. It's her…Clare." Her mother. Screaming her lungs out. At least it was a woman…although maybe it was one of the victims. But the sound was more mature somehow. And she was screaming words that Olivia couldn't make out.

"Why did you hide in the closet?"

She didn't want to talk about it but she couldn't resist answering him. His voice drew her. Made her want to lean into the strength he offered.

"Because it was the only place to hide and she told me to hide there. To take my sisters and stay in the closet until the monster was gone."

"Clare told you to do this?"

He knew the answer. Why did he ask? "Yes. Clare."

"Was Clare frightened when she told you this?"

"Yes…" Olivia's head ached with trying to remember. "She was always frightened of the monster. He did bad things."

That she recalled those sensations so vividly gave her pause. She inclined her head and listened to the voice whispering through her mind. Soft, gentle. And another sound… the humming. Olivia couldn't place the tune but it was so familiar. What was the name of that song?

"Did you see or hear Rafe?"

The question startled her. No, she didn't see her father. He was…he was…she didn't know. There was nothing. No feelings whatsoever. She shook her head. "I don't see or hear him in the dreams. And I don't feel him." She turned to St.

James. "What do you think that means? That I was totally disconnected from him? Emotionally disengaged?" People did that as a self-protection. Could that be why she didn't remember him?

Then again, she didn't exactly remember Clare. It was more a feeling that the woman's voice was her mother's.

"You should try and get another hour's sleep. It's barely four o'clock. It's going to be a long day."

He was right, she knew. But the idea of closing her eyes and going back to the dark place held no appeal whatsoever. "I'm not so sure I can do that. Maybe if you help me relax." There was no way to miss the glint of sexual interest in his eyes. She cocked an eyebrow. "I mean, tell me a story, St. James. About you. I know almost nothing about you." The idea that he was interested warmed her, filled that nasty void the nightmare had left in her chest. God, she hated those damned dreams.

"All right."

To her dismay, which she hoped didn't show, he moved back to his own bed.

"I grew up in Dallas. Studied criminology in college and went on to be a cop. Made it all the way to detective lieutenant before I walked."

She had him figured for a cop. She'd watched enough of them in the courtroom giving testimony. "Why'd you walk away from your career?" Like she had any room to talk. She'd walked away from law school barely a year shy of graduation.

He relaxed against the headboard, his hands clasped behind his head. The position forced the cotton tee to mold to his well-muscled body. "We'd take them off the streets and hotshot attorneys would put them right back on the street. I got sick of it and decided to go where I could do more for the victim, rather than wasting the taxpayers' money."

She shot him a speculative look. His expression shifted to

one of understanding, then contrition. "I work in a law firm that specializes in putting *them* back on the street."

"Sorry about that." He shrugged. "But it's true far too often."

"I know what you mean," she confessed. "Sometimes it's not fair, but it's the way our justice system works." Attorneys had no choice but to represent their clients to the best of their abilities—even when they discovered they were guilty.

"Why didn't you finish law school?"

She shouldn't be surprised he'd asked. He knew everything else about her. "I just decided one day that I didn't want that ultimate responsibility. It's kind of like choosing to be a nurse over being a doctor. You still get to help the sick and injured, but you don't have to carry the load when it comes to the politics and business side of the job. I get to counsel clients to a degree. I do lots of volunteer work. The boundaries are a little different. I have more freedom than my boss." And the truth was she'd chickened out. Deep inside she'd felt she wasn't worthy. Maybe now she understood why.

"You have any siblings? Parents still alive?" she asked him.

"One sister. Two parents. We get together on holidays and birthdays. We're all busy."

The tiniest hint of sadness tinged his voice. "You should make it a point to get together more often." Again, she had no room to talk.

He rolled onto his side and fixed those blue eyes on her. "I'll be sure to do that. You should, too."

"Touché." She managed a smile. "G'night."

He switched off the light. "G'night."

Chapter Nine

Polunsky Prison, 8:55 a.m.

Victoria leaned forward and peered at the crowd gathered around the gate of the prison. "Wait before you make the turn, please," she said to her driver.

"Yes, ma'am. It looks as though every media outlet in Texas has descended upon the prison. And those picketers don't look too happy. To make that turn, ma'am, we'd be forced to drive right through the worst of the crowd."

Unfortunately, he was all too correct. Dozens of news vans lined the road. Hundreds of people carrying signs and shouting had crowded the prison entrance. Her cell chimed and she reached into her purse to find it without taking her eyes off the massive crowd. She checked the screen. Warden Prentice. "Good morning. It appears you have an onslaught this morning. What's going on?"

"We believe Rafe Barker got word to a reporter that his case was being reviewed by a celebrated private investigations agency. A reporter from Austin called to demand an interview with me as well as Barker and when I denied his request he went public. This is only going to get worse."

The situation was not a completely unexpected turn of events. Victoria had anticipated the news would leak in time, though she had hoped it would be later rather than sooner.

"How did Barker get word to this reporter?" No mail left the prison unscreened. No calls or visitors got in without the warden's knowledge. After Weeden had smuggled out the letter from Barker to Victoria, all prison employees had been warned again that such behavior would not be tolerated.

Yet, someone inside had to have gotten the word out.

"Have you determined the source of the leak?" she prompted when Prentice remained silent. The prison staff with access to Barker was limited. Learning the identity of the culprit shouldn't prove difficult.

"At first I was certain it had to be someone from your agency. There are only four on staff with access to Barker now. But certain discrepancies in their statements changed my mind. No one has admitted to delivering his message, but we believe it was one of the two guards. I suspect one or the other will confess eventually but the damage is done."

"I'm just outside the gate, beyond the media and protest encampment. Is my meeting with Barker still on?" Whatever Barker had to say to her might or might not be relevant, but Victoria had questions for him. Demands, actually. She refused to play any more of his games. Admittedly, he had her at a disadvantage. It wasn't as if she could walk away from the case. Until this was over, Sadie, Laney and Olivia had to be protected. And the idea that Clare needed help, too, wouldn't be shaken from the fringes of Victoria's thoughts.

"That's why I'm calling you," Prentice explained. "Barker announced five minutes ago that he won't see you."

Victoria absorbed the ramifications of that statement for a moment before responding. "Did he provide a reason for this sudden change of heart? He was the one who demanded the meeting in the first place."

She asked the question knowing there would be no reasonable explanation. Rafe Barker was playing a game and she had just fallen into his trap.

"He refused to say anything more." The warden's hiss of frustration echoed across the line. "He's toying with us all, Victoria. He has what he wants now—whatever the hell that is—and he's going to sit back and relish the show until he's either executed or the governor grants a stay."

Prentice was perhaps more right than he knew. "He has a plan, I'll grant you that," she acknowledged. "But I don't believe that plan involves sitting back and waiting for anything. There's more coming. We simply haven't felt the repercussions of it yet."

"We have him on suicide watch. Not that I feel he intends himself harm. To the contrary. I'm fully expecting a final hoorah of some sort. I just hope it doesn't involve a full-on riot in my prison. At this point, I recognize that Barker, despite his decades of silence, has an influence here I never suspected for a second."

"You're aware, I'm certain," Victoria felt compelled to mention, "that an attorney in San Antonio is petitioning for a stay of execution."

"The state D.A. called me an hour ago. I'm sure it'll be breaking news before noon."

"Please keep me advised of any developments involving Barker." Victoria hoped he'd done all the damage within his power for now. But evil knew no boundaries. And she was fully convinced that Rafe Barker was far more evil than he asserted his wife to be.

Whether Clare was equally heinous was yet to be seen. It would seem, in light of recent events, that she was squarely on that path, whether by her own accord or not. If she was innocent, at least in part, how long would it take her to know she was falling into the same trap a second time?

Victoria ended the call. "You can take me back home, Clarence. My appointment here has been cancelled."

"We may have a problem, ma'am."

An abrupt commotion on the road in front of the car drew Victoria's attention beyond the windshield. A throng of reporters were racing toward them. Just behind the reporters and their cameramen was a crowd of protesters, signs waving, voices raised in demonstration.

"I'm backing up, ma'am."

Victoria braced for the maneuvers she knew would be required to avoid the trouble roaring directly at them.

Clarence slammed on the brakes. Victoria twisted in her seat to see what had stopped his retreat. Another news van had arrived and stalled at an angle across the road, preventing their escape.

"I'm calling nine-one-one, ma'am."

"Unfortunately, that may be the only step at our disposal." Still, time would be required for the appropriate authorities to arrive.

Reporters pressed their faces and their microphones to the windows and shouted questions. Was the Colby Agency supporting a stay of execution for Rafe Barker? Had new evidence indicating his innocence been uncovered? Victoria tried to slow her respiration and to relax. She couldn't respond to their questions because she had no answers. Then came the inevitable angrily shouted slogans of the protestors.

None of that bothered Victoria. It was an unavoidable aspect of having made the decision to look into Rafe Barker's claims. It was the questions that eventually came that clamped like a vise around her heart.

Is it true that the Barker girls are still alive?

Chapter Ten

Broken Egg Café, Livingston, 9:30 a.m.

"Something's wrong." Olivia peered out the large plate-glass window but there was still no sign of Keisha Landers. Their appointment had been for nine and this was the only Broken Egg Café in Livingston so there was no misunderstanding.

"You want to try her cell again?"

Olivia didn't see the point. She'd called both her cell and her office three times in the past half hour. The receptionist had no idea where Keisha was. She hadn't come into the office that morning. Worry dug its claws deep into Olivia's ribs, making it difficult to breathe.

"If we don't hear from her soon," St. James began, "we should speak to her employer and get the number for a family member we can call. Maybe there's been a family emergency."

Olivia knew what he was really thinking but she didn't want to go there. With the bombing of her car, there was no way around considering the possibility that something had happened to Keisha. She could be in a hospital somewhere… or worse.

Evidently noting her distress, he added, "I sent Simon a text and had him check with the local police to see if any accidents or other incidents involving Landers had been reported. Nothing so far."

Olivia appreciated his effort but she still couldn't relax. Not until she knew for certain. The buzz of his cell phone vibrating on the table sounded at the same instant that hers rang. That couldn't be good. Holding her breath, she blurted a hello.

"Olivia, I'm at the hospital."

Keisha Landers.

"What happened?" Olivia's gaze tangled with that of her protector, who was in deep conversation with his caller. Those blue eyes warned that the news on his end was equally grim.

"About three this morning someone broke into my house, set the place on fire and almost did me in. Actually I almost did myself in. The bastard made enough noise getting out of the house to wake the dead. I smelled the smoke and got out of the house immediately but I went back in for my father's papers. Dumb move. I ended up having to climb out a second-story window. The rose trellis didn't make for such a good ladder."

A chill seeped through Olivia. "Are you okay?" Keisha's voice sounded a little rusty and a lot tired but she was alive. Olivia should never have called her. She shouldn't have involved anyone else in this.

"Other than the smoke inhalation and a mild concussion, I'll live." Keisha blew out a big breath. "But my house is done. Worse, my father's papers are gone. Just gone. Everything. All that's left is what I gave you and your friend. Guard it with your life. I can't lose that, too."

"I will," Olivia vowed. "You have my word."

"I had a visit from a man named Simon Ruhl of the Colby Agency," Keisha went on. "Apparently they're investigating this case, too."

Olivia felt contrite that she hadn't been honest with her about St. James. But she'd given him her word.

Olivia didn't ask what Ruhl had wanted. Keisha assured Olivia that she would do as the doctor advised and stay in the hospital and rest. She urged Olivia to be very careful. "Someone doesn't want this investigation reopened badly enough to push just shy of murder."

As Olivia ended the call she considered the way the reporter had put her warning. Keisha was correct. Whoever was trying to stop this hadn't blown the car up while Olivia was inside or while anyone was nearby. He or she had waited for just the right opportunity to levy the most fear without hurting anyone. The same with Keisha's house fire. What perpetrator makes that much noise or forgets to disable the smoke detectors if murder by fire is the goal? Not only had her smoke alarms started wailing but the fire department had gotten a call from someone claiming to see smoke. The caller hadn't left a name.

That was a lot of extra trouble to go to in an effort to avoid unnecessary collateral damage unless the only intent was to destroy records that might confirm the investigation had been mishandled twenty-two years ago.

Clearly the person responsible had no intention of causing physical harm.

St. James ended his call, his attention still focused on Olivia. "The perp is either a cop or an ex-cop. Maybe a family member of one of the vics, but my money's on a cop." He withdrew his wallet and tossed several bills on the table.

Olivia's thoughts snagged on that move. "It's my turn to pay." She pushed his money to his side of the table and reached for her purse.

"Did you hear what I said, Olivia?"

She stared at him, blinked. "Yes. A cop." Apparently Simon Ruhl had gotten the story on the fire. Maybe even more insight from the cops investigating the case. She wanted to ask what he'd learned but she had a bad feeling where this was going.

The man seated across the table from her heaved a frustrated breath. "The only cops who would have a stake in this beyond a basic sense of justice are in Granger. Going there would be a bad move. Your reporter friend is in the hospital. Two of my colleagues just got out of the hospital. Another man is dead. Simon, my boss, has located a safe house where we can lay low until the dust settles."

Fury whiplashed her. "You mean until the next sixteen days have passed and Rafe Barker is executed? Or maybe until Clare and her twisted son hurt someone else? Is that what you mean, St. James?" She slapped her own money on the table. "Because if it is, our deal is off. I want the truth before Rafe Barker is dead."

He reached across the table and took her hand. She tried to pull away but he held on, his grip firm and strong yet gentle and unthreatening. "Listen to me. Just because this guy, whoever the hell is doing this, is playing it safe at the moment doesn't mean he'll keep it that way if he feels cornered or if desperation sets in too deep. Are you really prepared to sacrifice everything, even your life, to know the truth that you may already, in fact, know?"

If he hadn't been searching her eyes with such hope in his own, hope that she would understand he wanted to protect her, she might have grown even more angry. But he wanted to keep her safe. It was his job and that was important to him.

Part of her regretted that the job was likely his primary motive. Foolish. Foolish. "Last night I had that same nightmare I've had a thousand times before. I take my sisters into that closet because that's what our mother told me to do. I can hear her or someone, female and mature, not a child, screaming. I can feel the fear vibrating in my little sisters who aren't even old enough to understand what true fear is. And then when I think it's safe, I open the door and there's blood everywhere." Her fingers tightened around his. "I need to know what happened. Can you understand that?"

He gave a nod of agreement. It was vague, almost nonexistent, but at least he didn't say no.

"Then you won't try to stop me?" Her lungs seized, holding the air inside hostage. She had to do this. If he wouldn't help her, she hoped at least he wouldn't hinder her efforts.

"We had a deal, didn't we?" He gave her a smile, not his usual dazzler but brilliant enough to make her heart skip a beat. "Let's go." He glanced at the cash she'd left on the table lying next to the bills he refused to take back. "Our waiter's going to think you have a crush on him with a tip like that."

Olivia rolled her eyes and took back her hand. "Let's go before something else blows up." Like her libido. It was already smoking with the heat he'd generated just holding her hand. How in the world could she be attracted to a man, even one as good-looking and honorable as this one, at a time like this?

Bad genes. It was the only rational explanation.

Olivia hit the ladies' room first. The westward journey to Granger was well over three hours. If they wanted to arrive by midafternoon, they needed to limit stops. St. James had filled up the gas tank this morning so maybe there wouldn't be any stops at all.

After taking care of business, she studied her reflection as she washed her hands. No amount of concealer would take care of her dark circles. She hadn't had a decent night's sleep in ages. The nightmares had been a part of her life for as long as she could remember but the past couple of weeks they had become a nightly ritual. Maybe something trapped deep in her memory was attempting to resurface. Certainly the details in this latest nightmare had been more vivid.

Olivia supposed the shrink she'd seen two years ago was right. Talking about it had prompted more details. She grabbed a paper towel and dried her hands. It wasn't every night she had a big strong guy to hold her afterward and comfort her fears. That was another thing she decided wasn't so bad, having a partner in this.

Her boss was very supportive but only for the paperwork and the guidance. Nelson wasn't entirely convinced her quest was a good idea but he wouldn't deny her the leave from work to do what she felt she had to do. Funny, no matter that St. James was only doing his job, it felt like he actually cared what happened to her. Then again, she'd never had a body-guard. Maybe this was the usual routine.

"You really are pathetic, Liv." She shook her head at her-self. Had it been so long since she'd had a man, besides her father and her boss, in her life that she was overreacting to the mere presence of testosterone?

Maybe.

St. James waited for her right outside the ladies' room door. "Ready?" he asked.

"Definitely." As they moved toward the café exit, she of-fered him a piece of advice she had found handy on numer-ous occasions when time was of the essence as it was now. "Speed limits have a ten-mile-per-hour grace in my experi-ence. No cop is going to bother pulling you over and giving you a ticket for anything less than that."

"That," he said as he opened the door and the bell over-head jingled as if punctuating the word, "is because you're a woman. Trust me, I know."

Outside she sent him an annoyed look.

"And you're cute," he added.

Before she could rail at him for making such a sexist re-mark, he was striding toward the SUV. She hurried to keep up. "That is absolutely not true."

He performed his usual checks before unlocking and opening the vehicle. "You're right," he said when he at last opened the passenger-side door for her. "You're more than cute. You're very pretty in an uptight kind of way."

She settled into the seat and fumed. Uptight? She was not uptight. Her gaze crept down to the skirt and blouse she wore. Her choices had been limited. The navy skirt was not as tailored as the ones she usually wore. And the blouse was very plain. White, button-up. She never bothered with accessories like jewelry or scarves, and wore minimal makeup. She spent more time and money on her hair than anything else. It was too thick to manage easily. She kept it as short as she dared and still it was a handful. But there was nothing uptight about her.

"I resent your implication that I'm uptight." This she finally announced when they were well on the road toward Granger a full fifteen minutes later. Working up her nerve was not a task she generally had to perform. But everything was different with this man. "And your suggestion that women don't get tickets just because they're women isn't true. I've had lots of tickets."

"Statistics show," he argued, "that women do get fewer tickets than men. I should know, being an ex-cop and all."

"Maybe because we're better drivers."

He ignored the jab. "The other is just a figure of speech," he said, moving into the right lane and settling in to a nice speed just five miles per hour above the one posted.

"I dress and conduct myself in a professional manner. What's wrong with that? People have become far too lax in their manners, business and social."

"You have a point there." He glanced at her. Her cheeks flushed as if he'd stared at her a whole minute. "Do you want to hear what I really think or would you rather I kept my thoughts to myself since these particular ones have nothing to do with business?"

Olivia moistened her lips and ordered her heart to slow. "Why would you speak to me any other way besides frankly? We are a team, after all." Did two constitute a team? They certainly weren't a couple. Perhaps the better term was partnership.

"Whatever you say." He gave her another of those assessing sideways glances. "It just seems a shame to cover up so much of a gorgeous body like yours. The skirt could be a few inches shorter. Two or three buttons opened on the blouse would take the look from stiff and uncertain to relaxed and confident. The shoes are pretty damned awesome just the way they are."

Six or seven seconds were required for her to summon her voice after absorbing his suggestions. "You appear to have spent a great deal of time analyzing the way I look." She wasn't sure whether to be flattered or offended. What she did feel was too warm. She reached out and adjusted the vents and prayed the air coming from them would do the trick of lowering her body temperature.

"That's part of my job, too."

Surprised, she studied his profile. "To what end, Mr. St. James? Unless you'd rather not say. I wouldn't want you to give away any trade secrets." Were all men alike in that respect? They first measured a woman by the way she looked.

He sped up to move around a massive truck. "First off, my name is Russ. When you call me Mr. St. James it makes me feel old." He cut her a smile. "I'm not that old."

"Russ it is, then." Olivia stared straight ahead and wished she could unbutton the top two buttons of her blouse. But she would melt first. Not in a million years would she loosen her collar and have him think his suggestion had prompted the measure. She would be fine in a few minutes when he stopped talking in that deep, rich voice and he stopped sending her those sexy smiles.

"I assess the way people think and react in order to do my job. For instance, I know you get up at six every morning— usually," he qualified with another of those smiles tossed in her direction. "You go for a three-mile run on the same route, you shower for the same length of time, you eat a bagel or a cup of yogurt, get dressed and take the same route to the office."

"It's called a routine," she defended. "All organized people have one. That's why in two years I've never been late for work or court once." It was true. She did take the same route with her runs and her drive to the office. What of it?

"That kind of routine makes you an easy target. Even without a case like this on your plate, there are random assaults every day. Organized people make it easy for the bad guys."

Well, she would certainly never look at her routine the same way again. The idea stunned her. And it shouldn't have. She was well aware of the elements that made victims more vulnerable. But she had never considered herself a victim, which was the average person's first mistake. When had she stopped paying attention to her life to that degree?

"You wear gray on Mondays, navy on Tuesdays, brown on Wednesdays, and black both Thursdays and Fridays."

"I…" She stared down at the navy skirt she had chosen at the store in the wee hours of the morning without thought. "I hadn't really noticed." She was focused. Ambitious. And busy. She worked ten-hour days most of the time. What did he want from her? She was no clotheshorse. As long as she looked professional and well groomed, what difference did it make?

"You're totally different from your sisters."

The silence thickened while she steadied her bearings. Did he think he could make a statement like that and not follow it up with some explanation?

"What does that mean?" She didn't know her sisters. Why would she be anything like them other than in terms of genetics? The concept that she had two sisters and knew absolutely nothing about them still rattled her.

"Sadie runs a small ranch outside Copperas Cove. She

rescues horses. Laney owns and operates a classy saloon in Beaumont. She rescued the place from the wrecking ball and renovated it herself. Her old farmhouse, too. Both are never caught in anything but jeans and boots. I'll bet they don't own a single suit between the two of them."

Country girls. Rescuers. She did her share of rescue work, too. Only it was with legal advice and papers. She wore jeans in her off time. But never boots. She hated boots of any sort.

"What're they like beyond how they dress?" Part of her was afraid they wouldn't like her. That somehow they would blame her for not protecting them. She was the oldest. She should have done more…should have done better.

"They're good people, Olivia." He slowed for a bottleneck in the interstate traffic. "Hard workers, compassionate." He glanced at her, his gaze lingering long enough to send her pulse rate escalating. "Like you."

That his words pleased her so inordinately frustrated her.

"What do they look like now?" Would she recognize either one if she ran into her on the street? The thought tugged at something deep inside Olivia. It wasn't natural not to know one's family.

Russ picked up his cell from the console and passed it to her. "There's a photo of Sadie and Laney as well as Laney's son, Buddy."

"I have a nephew?" Had he mentioned that before? Olivia shouldn't have forgotten that no matter how caught up she was in this insanity.

"He's five. His father was the man we believe Weeden murdered."

He had told her that part, but somehow the fact that she had a nephew had been left out. Or maybe she'd been so caught up in the idea that Clare and Weeden had murdered someone that she'd missed the rest of what Russ said. With all that had happened in the less than twenty-four hours they had known each other it was a miracle they'd stayed on track with any kind of conversation.

She tapped the screen and opened the folder that contained the photos he'd either taken with his phone or that had been sent to him. The most recent photo was of herself going into the motel where she'd stayed her first night in Livingston. She looked tired. The next was of a little boy with brown hair and big brown eyes. He wore a cowboy hat and was all smiles. The woman who appeared on the screen next had the same blondish-brown hair as Olivia and the same eyes. Lisa— Laney, she amended. Her face was as familiar as Olivia's own. Her heart thundered as she moved to the next image. Sadie was beautiful. Her hair was more blond than brown and her eyes were green. She'd been so small the last time Olivia had seen her. But her face was familiar, too.

All these years they had been right here in Texas, only a few hours from Olivia. Anger stirred. Her adoptive parents should have told her. It was wrong that she and her sisters had grown up apart. As strangers.

Dealing with that hurt would have to wait for another time. She'd called her folks last evening and left a voice mail. She'd purposely chosen a time when she knew they wouldn't be home to avoid speaking to one or both. She'd told them she was fine and not to worry and that she would call again in a day or two. She hadn't mentioned the car. For now there was no need. They would worry if they didn't hear from her in any event. Who was she kidding? They were already worried and part of the reason was her fault. They were aware of her determination to understand the past and to find answers.

"May I forward these photos to my phone?" It would be nice to have recent photos of her sisters. At some point they would meet and maybe take the first steps toward a relationship. If either of them was interested.

"Sure." He sent her a telling look but kept the warning to himself.

"Don't worry, they're not evidence. I won't share them with anyone else until this is over." Did he think she was that desperate to prove her case?

Did she even have a case?

If she had deciphered her latest dream correctly, her father was a monster. But there was always the possibility that recent events had influenced her subconscious, causing her to lean in that direction. The only thing Olivia understood with complete certainty right now was that she had to know for sure. No speculating. No assuming. She needed the facts. And those facts would be found in one of three places. With Rafe and Clare, who were beyond her reach, and in Granger.

Someone there had to know something.

And if Russ was correct in his theory, someone there wanted the past and those facts to stay dead and buried.

Chapter Eleven

Granger, 2:20 p.m.
Where history lives...

Granger's town slogan seemed fitting in more ways than one, Russ mused. This was where the Barkers' history lived, buried under decades of pain and hatred. Reopening those old wounds was not going to be a pleasant task or an easy one.

He placed his hand on Olivia's arm and gave her a gentle shake. Her eyes opened, big and a rich brown that was even darker when she was angry or excited. She'd fallen asleep en route. He hadn't wanted to wake her. She'd needed the rest. But now he had no choice. Rest or no, she wouldn't be happy if he allowed her to miss anything beyond the Welcome to Granger sign he'd just passed.

"We're here."

She sat up, the seat belt tightened and she tugged to loosen it. For several seconds she studied the landscape. "Looks even smaller than it did the last time I came."

"Small, quiet," he agreed, "the kind of place where everyone knows each other's names."

"I imagine my name is one they would all like to forget."

The town's population was scarcely two thousand. At one time the area had been the hub of cotton trade with railroads ruling transit. Many of the old historic buildings remained, giving the town a true sense of the Old West.

"Do you want to start with Barbara Samson?" He remembered reading in one of the interview reports Landers had provided that Samson was one of the only two fairly close friends the Barker family had. Mrs. Samson had a daughter the same age as Olivia. The two girls had played together as kids according to the interview report but Olivia had no recall of the other little girl.

"Yes, she's a good starting place." Olivia dug through her bag until she came up with the folder she'd gotten from the reporter. "Maybe seeing her and photos of her daughter will trigger some of the memories I should have of that time."

"What was that address again?" Mrs. Samson still lived at the same address. Her husband had passed away and her daughter lived in Michigan now. If the lady was cooperative she could prove a good source of at least basic information.

"I'll enter it into the GPS," she offered. A few clicks later and they were following the turn-by-turn directions to the Samson home in a small neighborhood on the other side of town, not more than a couple of miles from the old Barker home place.

The small bungalow was surrounded by a yard cluttered with enough flowers to threaten the ability of the white picket fence to contain it. An old car encircled by last year's fallen leaves and looking as if it hadn't been driven since gasoline was under a dollar a gallon sat beneath a shade tree.

Russ parked in the driveway and shut off the engine. "Do you want me to get the lay of the land first?"

Olivia surveyed the home for another second or two. "I'm good." She reached for her door and hopped out. "As long as she doesn't start throwing rocks."

Russ chuckled. "Lucky for us there doesn't appear to be any handy." The lady's flower beds were mostly crowded with plants, no landscaping stones or pebbles in sight. He followed Olivia up the walk, taking it slow and giving her the time she required to absorb the details. The urge to ask if anything looked familiar nudged him but he kept the question to himself. She would tell him when she was ready.

They climbed the steps and crossed the wide porch. A sign warning that solicitors were unwelcome hung next to the door. Olivia glanced at him one last time before opening the screen door and knocking. The quiet inside suggested no one was home, but no sooner had the assessment formed than the knob turned and the door opened a few inches. He removed his wallet from his hip pocket just in case the woman of the house demanded official ID.

"You didn't see the sign?" the woman asked. She looked to be early sixties. Her gray hair was bundled atop her head and pink-rimmed glasses magnified her eyes, making them appear too large for her face.

"Ma'am, we're not selling anything. My name is Russell St. James." He showed her his ID. "I'm investigating a criminal case and I'd like to ask you a few questions if you don't mind."

The woman looked from him to Olivia. When she would have shifted her attention back to Russ, her gaze swung back to Olivia. "Do I know you?"

"My name is Olivia Westfield…." Olivia took a breath. "Barker. Olivia Barker. I lived in Granger as a child. You knew my parents, Clare and Rafe."

For two beats the woman stared in disbelief at Olivia then she promptly closed the door.

Not exactly the reception he'd hoped for. Russ raised his fist to knock but Olivia stopped him.

"Give me a few minutes," she urged. "Wait in the car and just…give me a few minutes."

He'd have a clear view of her so there was no reason not to

do as she asked. If he powered down the windows he could likely hear the conversation. "All right."

Olivia waited until Russ had climbed behind the steering wheel before she knocked again. "Mrs. Samson, I know this is startling but I need your help." Silence. "Please. I really, really need someone I can talk to." Olivia knocked again. "Please, Mrs. Samson, there's no one else. I really need your help."

The knob twisted and the door opened a few inches once more. "You and your sisters are supposed to be dead. Like the others. You show up here like a ghost and you expect me to just say come on in?"

That part was likely more shocking than merely startling to the poor woman. Olivia should have been more diplomatic.

"Yes, ma'am. I know. It was a shock to me, too. I had no idea that I was Olivia Barker until two weeks ago. My adoptive parents never told me. When I found out I was adopted, I launched a search for my biological parents. Imagine my shock when I discovered I was supposed to be dead."

The door opened a little wider. "I heard about your mama's release. You seen her yet?"

Olivia shook her head. "Not yet." She blinked at the burn in her eyes. Her emotions were getting the better of her. "Please, Mrs. Samson, I've come all this way and I'm finding nothing but dead ends. Will you please help me?"

"That your husband? I know you young women don't always take your man's name."

Funny, but Olivia wasn't taken aback by the suggestion of a husband. Russ was a nice guy. He would make a good husband for anyone looking for a mate. But Olivia wasn't in that market. Her personal life was far too screwed up to venture into relationship territory. Not that she'd ever had any luck there, anyway.

"He's a friend who's helping me sort this out." Olivia

glanced at the SUV where he waited. "May we come in and ask you some questions?"

"As long as he's not a reporter, I guess it'd be all right."

Olivia motioned for Russ to join them. "Have you been harassed by reporters about the case?"

"Not recently but back then…" She shook her head, sadness in her eyes. "It was awful around here for months. They were like vultures circling a rotting carcass."

When Russ was at her side, Olivia followed the woman into her home. She offered refreshments but Olivia declined, as did Russ. Forcing anything past the lump in her throat right now would be impossible.

When they were settled in her small living room, Mrs. Samson asked, "What do you want to know? I'm not sure I saw or heard anything that will satisfy you but I'll tell you what I remember."

"You lived here when the Barkers moved to town?" Olivia decided to start at the very beginning.

Mrs. Samson nodded. "They bought that old run-down farm years before you were born. Most folks around here had 'em figured for being a card shy of a full deck, if you know what I mean. It needed a lot of work. But in no time flat they had the old house dolled up and the barn turned into a clinic for animals. Everybody who got to know them liked them both immediately. They were that kind of folks. Kind, generous. We hadn't had a vet in this area before and it beat driving an hour to visit one in Austin. My old collie got sick and that's when I first met them. Your daddy had a knack with animals. Your mama was quieter. She mostly lurked in his shadow, but she eventually opened up around me when we ended up expecting at the same time."

"Mrs. Samson," Russ spoke then, "did the Barkers ever mention any relatives coming for a visit? Or did you ever see anyone else who might have been extended family? What we've been told so far is that they stayed mostly to themselves."

"They didn't bother with friends if that's what you mean. Being the only vet for an hour in any direction kept them pretty busy. And then the three of you," she said to Olivia, "came along. They were always busy. Your mama brought you to church most Sundays, but that's about it. If they had any relatives they never talked about them and none…ever visited. That I know of."

"You said the two of you got to know each other," Olivia reminded her. Her nerves were jumping with anticipation, particularly at her stumbling over the last part of her answer. She knew something more than she was sharing. Gaining her trust would take more time, which they didn't have. Olivia would have to go for persuasion and outmaneuvering. It was amazing what people would say when guided in just the right direction.

"As best anyone knew either of them, I suppose." The older woman frowned. "Clare seemed happy at first but things changed somehow those last few months before their arrests. They both changed. Became more withdrawn. Sort of antisocial."

"Surely," Olivia ventured, "having known them so long, you had your suspicions as to why they changed."

The lady stared at her hands a moment. "It started after… that other blonde showed up." She clasped and unclasped her hands as if the subject made her nervous. "But I didn't get the impression she was your mama's friend or a relative of any sort. Truth is, I only saw her a couple of times and then from a distance."

Olivia exchanged a look with Russ, and adrenaline burned through her veins. "What other blonde?"

"A woman. Looked a lot like Clare, maybe a little older. You might have thought she was Clare if you didn't pay close attention. I asked her about the woman once but she changed the subject. I mentioned it to the police after Clare and Rafe were arrested but they seemed to think I didn't know what I was talking about. Guess it was nothing. Considering what the two of them did, anyway."

"Ma'am, could the blonde woman have been Clare's cousin or sister? Maybe an aunt?" Russ ventured. Olivia understood that he was holding back. Putting words in the woman's mouth wouldn't help them find the truth.

"That was what I thought," Mrs. Samson explained. "Course I never saw the woman up close. The shape of the face was the same. Hair color was the same. About the same height and size as Clare. But Clare wouldn't talk about it so I figured it was one of those things best left alone."

Olivia struggled to control the trembling now rampant in her body. "You thought her presence was wrong somehow is that what you're saying?"

Her eyebrows reared up. "What else was I supposed to think? They'd started keeping to themselves as it was. After that woman showed up, I hardly saw Clare at all. There was never time for you and my Josie to play. It was very difficult for my daughter. Then after the news broke, I was thankful I hadn't let her go over there anymore."

"Your daughter visited the Barker home?" Russ asked for clarification.

Olivia held her breath.

"She played over there on numerous occasions." The woman kept her gaze on Russ as she spoke, carefully avoiding eye contact with Olivia. "The last time I took her over there, that's when I saw that other woman. The place was a mess. Not clean and neat like your mama usually kept it. Smelled bad, too. Like alcohol and cigarette smoke. Josie never went again and your mama never let you girls out of her sight even for a visit with me." Mrs. Samson shook her head sadly. "My Josie suffered terrible nightmares after we discovered what had been happening over there. She won't discuss that time in her life to this day."

"Did she ever mention seeing or hearing anything that made her feel uncomfortable or frightened?" Russ pressed.

Olivia was holding her breath again, leaning forward slightly in anticipation of the answer.

Mrs. Samson cleared her throat. "You understand that I don't want my daughter involved in whatever is going on with that tragedy. This whole community suffered enough." She turned to Olivia then. "I truly do sympathize with your need for answers but if you pursue my daughter I will deny everything I've just told you."

"You have my word," Olivia assured her. "No one will ever know that any of what we discuss here came from you."

"Josie said you showed her the bedroom closet and explained that you and your sisters hid there when the bad things were happening." She clasped her fidgeting hands in her lap. "You showed her how your mother would pray for the bad things to stop. Your screaming and ranting, when you were mimicking her prayers, scared Josie and she didn't want to go back for a long time after that visit. But Clare took that decision out of our hands when she totally withdrew from everyone and everything."

Olivia's heart thudded so hard against her sternum she felt certain it would burst. "I…" She wet her lips. "I can't remember anything. I don't remember Josie."

For a moment Mrs. Samson sat very still just staring at Olivia, then she got up and crossed the room. She removed a photo album from a shelf and returned, but this time she sat down on the sofa next to Olivia. When she found the page in the album she was looking for, she reached beneath a photo and pulled out one that was hidden. She handed it to Olivia.

"I took that the last time the two of you played together.

It was just a few months before the arrests. You may keep it. Maybe it'll help you remember. I'm sorry I can't be of more help. Whatever went on in that house, Rafe and Clare kept their secrets from us all. Made the whole town feel guilty for not knowing what was going on over there."

Russ thanked Mrs. Samson as they moved toward the door. Olivia hugged her and thanked her, as well, but the movements and words were by rote. She felt numb, mechanical. Deeply disturbed. The little girl in the photo, Josie, with the fiery red hair, was a total stranger. Olivia had no recall of her whatsoever, yet they stood side by side, arms looped over each other's shoulders. How could she not remember?

In the SUV, her fingers felt like ice as she slid the buckle of her seat belt into place. Russ backed out of the driveway and rolled away from the house and the woman Olivia could not remember. They drove through the town that she had no memory of seeing prior to her recent visit with the police here.

It was all gone. Vanished. Blocked away as if it never happened. But it had happened. Her parents, one or both, had brutally murdered more than a dozen young girls. She and her sisters had been in the house when those tragic events occurred and she recalled nothing but the darkness…the screaming and some vague humming.

"Take me to the house." She had driven by it the last time but she hadn't possessed the nerve to stop, much less get out.

"It may be sealed as a crime scene after what happened there this past weekend."

Laney/Lisa, her younger sister, had come there to find her son, who Clare and Weeden had taken. There had been a shootout and a Colby Agency investigator had been shot. She'd seen some fleeting mention of the shooting on the news but it hadn't been in the major papers. Russ had told her about it, giving her details the news had not.

"I don't care. I need to see that closet."

He didn't protest further. He drove. Olivia closed her eyes, unable to deal with any more visual stimulation. And she needed to think. Who was the blonde Mrs. Samson had seen? Could she have been Janet Tolliver, Clare's sister? If there had been another woman at the house besides her mother, wouldn't she remember that? Why had this news not triggered anything new? Why couldn't Olivia remember her one friend, Josie? Or her friend's mother, Mrs. Samson? She rubbed her thumb across the images in the photograph she held but couldn't bring herself to open her eyes and look at the smiling faces, the seemingly happy faces. But she hadn't been happy. A happy child remembered her childhood.

Olivia wasn't sure how many minutes passed. One or ten, the time ran together in one clump of misery. When he braked to a stop and shut off the engine she opened her eyes. The big old house loomed before her, its white siding grayed with age and neglect. The house sat a good distance off the road, bordered on either side by massive trees that shaded its rusting tin roof. Beyond the house she could barely see a portion of another roof, its shape barnlike. The clinic.

The sound of his door opening prodded her from the uncertainty paralyzing her. She opened her door and climbed out. The ankle-deep grass rushed across the yard and surrounded the house with its crippled porch that leaned to one side. Most of the windows had been partially boarded up, giving an even creepier feel to the place. The air was still and silent as if it too waited for her next move.

So much tragedy had happened here. It was a miracle the stench of evil didn't linger in the air. She walked toward the porch, dragging the thick, humid air into her lungs. On the porch the floorboards creaked as she followed Russ to the door.

"We should check the back door. Entering from the rear will give us cover from anyone passing by."

She nodded in agreement. His words didn't really pene-
trate. She was drinking in the details. Abandoned birds' nests
and cobwebs decorated the sagging porch ceiling. The posts
and rails were in bad need of repair and no longer provided
the intended structural integrity.

As they moved around the rear corner of the house, Olivia
stalled. An old swing set waited beneath one of the ancient
trees. The colors were faded and rust had overtaken parts but
it seemed familiar. Laughter whispered through her mind.
They had played here, she and her sisters.

The barn-turned-clinic sat several yards back from the
house. In between was a rock-skirted well. The old-fashioned
sort with a rusty, banged-up bucket and a frayed rope. An
old crank handle remained where someone had left it the last
time water had been drawn.

Another massive tree had grown up against the house as
if it had been small when the house had been built and no
one had noticed it taking over. Limbs pressed against the siding. The sound those limbs would make when the wind blew
scraped across her mind. The sound had terrified them as
kids. An abrupt Texas summer storm would have it rubbing
and clawing at the house as if it were intent on getting inside.

His weapon in hand, Russ led the way across a screened-
in back porch and into the house through the rear entrance.
So far they had seen no sign of the house being sealed as a
crime scene. The once boarded up door stood ajar as if no
one cared who entered.

Inside there were more cobwebs and dust covered most
every surface, including the worn linoleum floor. The table
had been wiped free of dust and the remains of sandwiches
that would soon be moldy lay on paper plates. A chest-type
cooler sat on the floor. Clare and Weeden had been here for
more than a simple visit. Apparently they'd been hoping to
use the place as a hideout.

"Stay behind me," Russ instructed as he moved forward into the darker interior.

A flashlight switched on. She hadn't realized he'd brought one along. Between the musty smell and the creeps this place was giving her, she was glad at least one of them was thinking clearly. The utter silence was spine chilling. She hugged herself and stayed as close to him as possible.

The hallway from the kitchen led to the front door. Off the hall as they neared the front door were two large rooms, one on either side. The stairs to the second floor looked less than reliable even in the dim lighting.

Russ moved carefully up the stairs, checking each tread as he went. At the top of the stairs was a bathroom. To the right was a single door. Her parents' room. She didn't have to go inside; the certainty was palpable. The sensations of betrayal and deception were nearly overwhelming. She did not want to go in there. To the left were two more doors. One that led to a room on the back side of the house and one that opened to a room on the front.

The room on the front was just a bedroom. A single bed and a bureau. She hesitated before moving back into the hall. For a long moment she stood at what she assumed was a closet door. Her hand shaking, she reached out and opened it. Inside were ropes and chains. Twisted articles of clothing. She closed the door. Didn't want to analyze what that meant.

Down the hall was the final room, the one that backed up to the big tree. She opened the door and sensations and images assaulted her senses. The room was pink. There was one full-size bed, a dresser and toys scattered across the wood floor. Olivia could hear the tree branches rubbing the house...she could smell the scents of the baby shampoo her mother had used to wash their hair and the soap she'd used on their skin.

The bubbles and the splashing water as they bathed together felt as warm and real as if it were happening at that very moment. She could see the images as plainly as if she were watching a movie. Clare would laugh with them, scrub their shivering bodies with a big fluffy white towel. Then she'd dress them in matching pajamas and usher them off to bed.

They would play and giggle beneath the covers until they fell asleep…only to be awakened hours later by the screaming.

Olivia turned to the closet. Their hiding place. The secret place that protected them from the monster. She walked across the room and reached for the knob. Her hand shook.

Russ was suddenly beside her, his hand on the small of her back. "I'm right here," he murmured.

She had never in her life been more relieved to have backup. "Thank you."

Olivia opened the door and Russ ran the flashlight over the small space. Bead board walls and ceiling, like the rest of the house. Cobwebs and dust covered every surface. It was so much smaller than she remembered…cramped.

She turned to Russ. "I need to do something." She moistened her lips and grappled for the courage. "Stay right here, please." The notion of being left alone in this place was abruptly terrifying.

"I'm not going anywhere," he promised.

Olivia stepped inside the closet and pulled the door closed. Total darkness consumed her. She shut her eyes and inhaled deeply. This had been their safe place. The monster couldn't touch them here. It had seemed so big as a child…like a room, but it was nothing more than a closet. A tiny closet where three children had cowered from the danger.

The whoosh of fear came out of nowhere. Suddenly Olivia was five again and her sisters were huddled against her sobbing softly, their little bodies shivering with fear. She couldn't block the screaming…the words of supplication that she now recognized as fervent prayer. The blackness started to spin and spin and spin. Olivia couldn't catch her breath.

She would see the blood when she opened the door. It was always there.... She saw it every time in her dreams. She didn't want to open the door. Didn't want to see the blood. But if doing this would trigger more memories, she had no choice.

Her hand shaking, she reached out and twisted the knob. The latch snapped, the door creaked open and her mother smiled at her. She was wearing a pink dress with little white flowers. Her hair was long and blond, her feet were bare. She looked young and pretty, the way she had when Olivia was five.

"Don't worry, baby, it's okay now."

Olivia's gaze lowered, followed as her mother got down on her hands and knees on the floor. There was a bucket of sudsy, steaming water. Her mother reached into the bucket and pulled out a scrub brush and started rubbing at the blood pooled on the scarred wood floor.

"It was just an accident, baby, don't be afraid."

The room started to spin harder and faster and then it went black.

Chapter Twelve

Russ caught Olivia before she crumpled to the floor. The flashlight bounced and rolled, sending its beam of light circling around the dimly lit room.

"I've got you." He gathered her into his arms, but she stirred and started to struggle. "You're okay, Olivia. We're getting out of here."

Olivia stopped struggling and rested her head against his shoulder. He glanced at the flashlight but decided it wasn't worth the trouble.

He angled and sidled out the door of the bedroom she and her sisters had shared long ago, then he moved more quickly down the hall. The stairs he took more slowly since, under their combined weight, the treads gave a little more than he would have liked. By the time they reached the kitchen he was mentally cursing himself for bringing her here. The dampness of her tears on his neck made him want to drive to the prison and beat the hell out of her monster of a father.

A deep breath wasn't possible until they were safely outside in the fading sunlight. There were still a couple of good hours of daylight left but he had no desire to hang around here a minute longer. Olivia had had enough for one day.

She lifted her head and swiped at her eyes. "I'm fine now."

He settled her onto her feet and she swayed. "You sure

about that?" She looked about as fine as a rosebush after a hailstorm. Shaky, torn and frazzled.

After a deep breath, she nodded. "My mother was cleaning up blood from the floor and she kept telling me it was just an accident and for me not to be afraid." She pressed her hand to her stomach. "The things that happened here…" She stared up at the old house. "I can't remember specific events but even in my five-year-old mind I recognized it was bad… really bad."

She hugged her arms around her middle and turned away. "My mother might not have killed any of those little girls but she cleaned up the mess at the very least. She enabled him and this—this house of horrors."

"You can't be sure of those snippets of memory," he reminded her gently. No matter whether she said it out loud or not, some part of her needed to believe that one or the other of her biological parents was inherently good. No child wanted to feel they'd come from pure evil, and that little five-year-old girl who still lived deep inside Olivia didn't want to, either.

"I'm sure enough," she argued. "I'm certain of something else, too." She fixed a determined gaze on him. "I want to see the place where they found the bodies."

That really was a bad idea. Before he could stop her she was already marching toward the woods. "Don't put yourself through that, Olivia. It won't change anything." It was possible she could remember more but was it worth the torture? Would it change the facts and how those facts impacted her heart and her life?

She whipped around and glared at him. "I don't know why they didn't burn this place down." She shifted her furious look to the house. "It shouldn't still be standing. That's what I know for an absolute certainty."

"The families of several of the victims bought the place

and closed it up so they could ensure no one ever lived here again. Not in this house or one that was built in its place."

"What was the point in that?" She flung her arms upward in frustration. "It's here. A tragic monument to murder. Can't they see that?"

Russ couldn't pretend to know how those families felt so he offered what he could. "Maybe they believe that some part of their children's spirits will forever be attached to this place. Maybe they can't bear the idea of burning down that possibility. This was the last place they were alive. Maybe the survivors need that connection. Or maybe they just hope some kind of answers will eventually be found here about the remains still unaccounted for."

Olivia shook her head and turned to the woods. She was determined to go in there and see what she could find. He didn't try to stop her; the attempt would be futile. Keeping an eye out for trouble, he followed. It was his job to keep her safe but she wasn't making it easy.

The canopy overhead was thick enough to block a good portion of the sun. A few streaks of daylight managed to filter through the mass of trees. The former gravesites were located only a couple hundred yards from the clinic, directly behind the house. But twenty years of underbrush and saplings had obscured them. He felt fairly certain she wouldn't find what she was looking for but she needed to see that for herself.

She wound through the trees, plowing through the brush as if her life depended on accomplishing her goal. Emotion was driving her and nothing he said or did would make this right. As the oldest, the past was a far greater burden for Olivia. Her sisters had accepted what they could not change and appeared to be moving on. The task would be far more difficult for the oldest. She felt a sense of responsibility that wouldn't be shaken quite so easily.

As much as Russ wanted to be sensitive to that, lingering

in the woods this way made keeping her safe far more difficult for him and her safety needed to be priority one just now.
As vigilant as his surveillance, there were too many hiding
places for trouble out here for his liking.

"Come on, Olivia, too much time has passed. You're not
going to find what you're looking for and we need to be on
our way before dark."

She turned on him, directing her frustration and her anger
his way. "You don't understand how this feels." She started
forward once more. "I need to do—" She stumbled, went
down face-first.

He cut through the brush and was at her side before she
could drag up onto her hands and knees. "We should go now.
You've put yourself through enough for today. We'll come
back early in the morning if you still feel this is necessary."

Ignoring him completely, she swept the leaves away from
the ground in front of her. "I think I found something."

A flat stone, partially buried in the earth, had a kneeling
angel carved into its surface. He hadn't read anything about
the grave sites having been marked. Maybe one or more of
the families had done this later. All the remains found had, of
course, been removed and claimed by the families for proper
burial. But this place was where their children's remains had
rested for months and years.

The reality had his gut churning. All that time those girls
were missing, their families and the police searching and
searching, hoping against hope they were still alive. And they
were right here…in a monster's backyard.

Olivia sat back on her heels. "Oh, my God. This is it." She
scanned the woods around her. "The remains were discovered
in unmarked graves very close together." She gestured to the
area in front of her. "See how there aren't any big trees, just
smaller ones? This is it."

On their hands and knees, they prowled through the brush,

feeling for more of the stones. "Found one," he called out to her. Their gazes met across the small span and his heart lurched. Her face looked so pale. Her heart was breaking for the young girls who had been buried here, their lives cut short by an evil bastard.

The evil bastard who was Olivia's father.

It was almost dark by the time they found the last one. Olivia's hands and knees were covered in dirt. The skirt she'd bought last night was ruined and dotted with decaying leaves but she didn't care.

Eight stones for eight little angels who had once rested here.

At some point in the past two decades the families had stopped coming and to this unholy place. They'd been forced to move on. Their daughters were gone and coming back here wasn't going to give them the answers they sought.

Whatever she found, Olivia wondered if it would give her any peace.

She stood and brushed off her skirt and attempted to do the same to her knees. Not happening. The dirt might very well be hiding the fact that both knees were skinned from scrubbing around on the ground.

She should be more like her sisters and dress in jeans more often, she thought. Her hands paused in their work. Had her sisters come here and looked at this place? Laney had come to find her son, but had she taken a long, hard look? Had they studied the sickening details of this rotting monument to their painful history? If they hadn't maybe it was better for them. If they remembered nothing at all about this place and that time they were far better off in Olivia's opinion.

There was nothing here worth remembering.

Russ walked over to her and reached for her hand. His were as filthy as her own but their strength and warmth felt good to hold onto. The knees of his jeans would never be the same. His black shirt hadn't handled the abuse well, either. He'd left the Stetson in the SUV, which had probably saved it from a similar fate.

"I'm taking you out of here even if I have to throw you over my shoulder and carry you."

He meant what he said, too. Her eyes had long ago adjusted to the scant and sporadic sprinkling of light, allowing her to see his expression. "You won't get any argument out of me this time." She was beat. As crazy as it sounded, she felt as if she actually had accomplished something important. She had acknowledged those who'd lost their lives here and she'd needed to do that. She'd needed to feel the dirt between her fingers and to know that despite the insanity of this hellacious place she had survived. Whatever the truth was, she owed it to those who had not survived to find it and reveal it to the world.

He tightened his fingers on hers. "Let's go. It'll be dark soon. We've pressed our luck already."

With him leading, she hung on to that big strong hand of his and lamented her foolish fetish for high heels. Not that she'd exactly planned things this way. The decision to search for those former grave sites had been her going with her heart instead of her brain for the first time in a really long time.

Once they reached the yard she realized how late it actually was. The sun had dipped low in the sky and a crisp breeze had kicked up. Limbs of the old tree at the back of the house were swiping back and forth against the neglected siding, making the sound she knew so well from her dreams. She hadn't precisely known what the sound was until she came here today and saw the tree. Many things about her dreams had cleared in her mind.

But she was no closer to the truth than she had been yesterday. She drew Russ to a stop midway across the backyard. When his full attention rested on her, she asked the question she'd set aside to come here. "Do you think the other woman Mrs. Samson thought she saw was Janet Tolliver?"

"That was my thinking," he offered. "We don't have any photos of Janet when she was young. If the agency had suspected who she was immediately after her murder, we might have been able to get a photo from her great-niece. The house she lived in has been packed up and everything moved to storage so it won't be so easy now. I sent an update to Simon via text. He's going to contact the niece and see if she can help us."

"Could she have been hiding out here? Involved in the murders? Why wouldn't Clare or Rafe mention that at trial?" Of course, Rafe hadn't said a word but Clare had said plenty. Never once had she mentioned another female presence in the house. Olivia had read a copy of the trial transcript and there was nothing there about another woman, blonde or otherwise.

"We may never know. There's always the chance that Mrs. Samson was mistaken."

"Do you think we should go against Mrs. Samson's wishes and contact her daughter?" Olivia didn't want to hurt the woman or her daughter but this was too important to ignore what had been swept under the rug.

"I think we should do whatever we have to do."

Olivia's chest welled with gratitude. As much as she respected her boss, he was a good boss and a friend. But he felt Olivia's digging into all this was a mistake. Having this man on her side meant a great deal. "Thank you."

Confusion lined his face. "What for?"

"Supporting me as well as playing the part of protector. And if," she said before he could respond, "you say it's your job I might just punch you." He had a smudge of dirt on his jaw. His blond hair was tousled. As ridiculous as it sounded, he looked good all messy and unpolished.

"I won't pretend to know how difficult this is," he said in

the gentle voice that was so unexpected from a big cocky-looking cowboy like him. "But I know when a person needs a real friend. Today, you needed a friend. In addition to a bodyguard." That prized grin spread over his face.

She reached up hesitantly. "You have dirt…right here." She wiped it away with the pad of her thumb. "There."

For a long time he stared straight into her eyes. And for the first time in too long to recall she wished for more. Most of the time when she got those stares of longing she just turned away. But not this time. This time she wanted him to look his fill and then she wanted him to kiss her. To put those powerful arms around her and hold her tight the way he had when he'd carried her out of that awful room.

"What I want to do right now is definitely not part of my job," he said softly.

"I'm sure it's after five o'clock." She moistened her lips. That he watched the move so intently had her heart racing. "Even a bodyguard has to have a break."

His arms went around her and his mouth crushed onto hers. She didn't have time to catch her breath but she didn't care. She wanted to feel something real. Something warm and alive. She wanted to feel him holding her this way, his mouth devouring hers with the same intensity she'd seen in his eyes.

When he at last drew his lips from hers, resting his forehead against hers, he whispered, "I'm going to need a lot longer than a quick break to do this right." He inhaled a heavy breath. "And unfortunately now is not a good time to be that distracted."

The way his hands cupped her bottom, keeping her pelvis pressed solidly against his warned that he wasn't happy about the choice but it was the right one to make. The contact also revealed that he wanted a whole lot more than just a kiss. Anticipation swelled inside her.

She licked the taste of him from her lips, couldn't help herself. "As soon as this is done, I expect you to make good on the implication your hips are making, Mr. St. James."

"Count on it."

He dragged his arms free of her body, maintaining the intimate contact for as long as possible before turning to head to the SUV. That he held on to her hand did strange things to her pulse rate.

As they neared his SUV, he stalled. "What the hell?"

Olivia leaned around him and tried to determine the problem. Her gaze latched onto the front tires. She gasped. Both were flat. They walked around the SUV. The rear tires were flat, as well. He crouched down to inspect first one, then next on the driver's side.

"Someone isn't happy to see us."

"Slashed?" That was her first thought.

He stood, gave her a nod as he withdrew his weapon and took a long look around. "I'll put in a call to my motor club and see if they can get someone out here ASAP."

Ice filling her veins, Olivia turned back to the house. She sure hoped so. Staying here after nightfall was not something she could do. She hugged her arms around herself in an effort to block the cool breeze. Out here in the middle of nowhere it might take some time to get roadside service. Her fingers tightened into fists. Who would do this? Could have been Tony Weeden, maybe. He and Clare could be lurking about. Olivia surveyed the property and then the woods and pastures that bordered the road for as far as the eye could see. They could be watching and waiting for the cover of darkness.

"You think whoever did this is still out there somewhere?" She shuddered. Russ was with her and he had a weapon.

"Maybe." He surveyed the area again. "Depends on if it was Weeden or just some local who wants us to know he isn't happy we're here. One thing you can count on, if whoever did this had wanted to do either of us harm he had the perfect opportunity while we were in the woods. Chances are he did this and got the hell out of here."

Olivia stayed close to him as he made the necessary call. If anyone was watching them they were hidden in the woods. The road was deserted in both directions. Another of those creeping shivers rushed over her skin.

"They can have someone here in an hour," he announced, drawing her from the troubling thoughts. "Give me a minute to check it out and if I don't find any hidden explosives or other anomalies, we'll load up and have some of those snacks and bottled water I have tucked in my backpack while we wait."

Her stomach responded to the suggestion. She hadn't thought of food in hours. "I hope you have potato chips."

"Never leave home without them."

Her lips curved into a smile. How he did that under the circumstances was beyond her. He spent a good long while examining the undercarriage of the vehicle, then beneath the hood. He'd scrounged up another flashlight from beneath the front seat. While he checked the SUV, she kept an eye out for any movement.

When he was satisfied that it was safe, he unlocked the SUV and opened her door. While she made herself comfortable, he opened the door behind her and rummaged through his backpack.

"Just what the lady ordered." He passed her a bottle of water and a bag of chips.

When he'd rounded the hood and climbed behind the wheel, she asked, "Do you think someone followed us here?"

"Don't think so. I kept an eye on the traffic behind us as we neared Granger. No one followed us from the Samson home. My guess is she called someone and mentioned that we were here."

"Someone like a family member of one of the victims?"

She downed a gulp of water to chase the salty chips. "Or someone like a local cop?" Her money was on the cop. The two she'd attempted to interview had let her know in no uncertain terms that they were not happy with her digging.

"Hard to say. Slashed tires are far less troubling than having automobile parts end up all over the yard."

She could vouch for that. "But how would anyone, even the police, know we were here unless they got a call? Mrs. Samson is the only person who knew we were in town."

He reached into his pocket and retrieved his ringing cell. A glance at the screen and he said, "It's Simon."

Olivia found herself holding her breath as she listened to his side of the conversation. Didn't sound like the kind of news he'd wanted to hear. His voice had turned somber. His profile looked grim.

He ended the call and placed his phone on the console. "We're about to have company."

"The police?" How she made that leap based on a call from the Colby Agency, which was in Houston, she would never know.

"Not yet, but they'll be next. Someone leaked to the press that you're here. As in *here.* Several stations from surrounding areas are en route. And we're stranded."

Olivia stared at the house. She would not go back in there. "How do you know the police will be here next?" The salty taste of the chips turned sour on her tongue.

"The petition for the stay of execution just hit the wire. Word is spreading like wildfire. The local cops will feel compelled to intervene in the event that reporters aren't the only folks who show up out here before roadside assistance arrives."

"You mean like protesters?" That was a strong possibility if her presence was known.

"Yep. And irate family members of the victims." He

showed her the depth of his concern with his eyes. "Some won't take this well. You need to be braced for that."

For two weeks she had been certain she was braced for anything. Now she wasn't so sure.

Chapter Thirteen

8:45 p.m.

"She's on the news."

Clare roused from the doze she had slipped into. She sat up on the side of the bed. "What did you say?" She and Tony had driven back to Houston, since fading into the background in a large city was far easier than in a small town. There were many more cheap motels to choose from, as well. No one asked questions in places like this.

"Olivia is on the news." Tony gestured to the television set. "She and the man from the Colby Agency."

Clare peered at the dim screen. The reception was quite terrible, leaving the images snowy and wavy. But he was right. It was Olivia. Her heart leaped. Her oldest.

The breath trapped in her lungs and twisted like a corkscrew. "She's at the house." She leaned closer still to the fuzzy images. "The police are there." Blue lights flashed against the night. "Do you suppose something has happened?"

"Listen and we'll find out," he snapped.

Tony had been very irritable this evening. She supposed his shoulder ached. But that was no reason to ignore her the way he had and then jump down her throat the first chance he got.

He'd been very withdrawn since the shooting. It was as if he blamed her. She hadn't told him to hurt anyone. If he hadn't shot at that man watching over Lisa—Laney, she called herself now—none of this would have happened. Maybe Clare could have spoken to her daughter and explained how they had rescued Buddy. But as it was Clare hadn't gotten the chance and she'd been terrified that Laney or her precious little boy would be hurt.

She dismissed the disturbing thoughts and paid attention to the reporter. Someone had damaged the vehicle Olivia and the man were driving. The police were there to protect them from further trouble, according to the reporter.

Then the woman launched into the breaking news that her station had learned that all three of the Barker girls were alive. The eldest, Olivia, had petitioned the courts for a stay of execution on her father's behalf.

The rest of the reporter's words were lost on Clare. How could Olivia be so foolish? Rafe should die! He should burn in hell for all eternity! Who had filled her head with such nonsense?

The Colby Agency. Olivia had only done this foolish thing after becoming involved with them. The Colby Agency was keeping Laney and Sadie out of Clare's reach.

She had to do something. Wilting onto the side of the bed, she twisted her fingers together to stop their shaking. How could she talk to her daughters if they were being kept from her? *He* had summoned the aid of this Colby Agency. He did not want her to succeed in bringing her girls together as a family again.

"You see what she's done?"

Clare jerked from her troubling thoughts. Tony was staring at her, his eyes wild with fury. "She's under the influence of that Colby Agency," Clare argued. "She's confused, that's all."

"She wants to hurt you," Tony challenged. "I'm the only one who really cares about you. Don't you see that?"

He had suggested that same nonsense after that man had

shot him. Clare didn't like when he talked that way. "I think we've gone about this all wrong. I should have called each one as soon as I was released from prison and told them the truth."

"How could you?" he mocked. "You didn't even know where they were until I beat it out of that old bitch."

He was right. Clare's hopes fell. Janet had tried to keep the truth from her. If not for Tony she would have had no idea where to look. As soon as she was released he had found Clare. He had known her release was imminent and he had made numerous arrangements. She had scarcely thanked him. How could she be frustrated with him now? He was only trying to protect her. He had told her over and over that none of the trouble in Beaumont had been his fault. Hadn't he gotten her away from that man who had been watching her in Copperas Cove? That Lucas Camp from the Colby Agency. Yes, her boy had helped her tremendously.

He had risked much to help her. He had given up his job and done whatever she needed. He'd had no control over the turn of events in Beaumont when Laney's child had been taken by his no-good father. Tony had rescued the boy.

Then that awful Colby Agency man had tried to cause trouble by interfering. No one would have been hurt if not for him. Tony was right. He had been protecting her. Rafe had hired the Colby Agency. They were on his side, which meant they were against Clare.

No one was ever going to believe the truth. She had no way to prove what really happened. Rafe had turned their home into hell. He and that whore sister of hers.

Rafe would take the truth to hell with him and Janet was already in hell. Perhaps if Tony had been more careful, Janet would still be alive and Clare could get the truth out of her. But he'd had to stop her interference. Janet had intended to warn the girls and threatened to make sure they never spoke to their mother. She would have, too. She would have done anything to ensure Rafe got what he wanted.

She had turned him into the monster he became. Her and her sexual deviance.

Clare wished she had ended her evil existence a long time ago. Before she ruined everything.

It was too late for that now. Clare had to focus on the future. She had nothing to take to her daughters in the way of proof of what she knew. Somehow she had hoped they would remember certain things. Particularly Olivia. She was the oldest and should have remembered something.

But she hadn't so far; otherwise she would not be taking her father's side. Perhaps her memories were blocked… buried. Too painful to look at. But she wanted to remember or she wouldn't have gone to the house in Granger.

She had to be searching for the truth whether she was conscious of it or not.

Clare had read a little about memory triggers. Smells often helped with recalling people and events. Sounds did, as well.

Hope bloomed in her chest and a smile lifted her lips. There might be hope. If only she had thought of this before.

"I want to go back to the house," she announced.

Tony glared at her as if she had lost her mind. "We can't go back there."

She stood, squared her shoulders. "We can and we will. There's something in the house I have to find."

He growled. "I hope it's worth going back to prison for."

He had no idea, but it was worth anything and everything. It might very well be her only chance.

Chapter Fourteen

The Boxcar Motel, Granger, 11:00 p.m.

Russ clicked off the television and paced the small room. His SUV wouldn't be ready until morning. Simon had ensured a rented sedan was delivered to the motel but it was too late to head back to Houston by the time it arrived. Russ didn't like the idea of staying the night in Granger, but it was the most reasonable option.

Tomorrow he was getting Olivia out of here. She'd put on a brave face throughout the ordeal of being bombarded by the reporters. The two police officers who had arrived to make the report had been less than sympathetic because Russ and Olivia had been trespassing. Russ had kept the part about going inside the house out of their statements. Spending the night in lockup for breaking and entering was about as appealing as going head to head with another flock of reporters. The investigating officers hadn't bothered to go beyond the first floor inside the house. Russ would have had a heck of a time explaining the flashlight he'd dropped in that bedroom.

To her credit, Olivia had fielded their questions with strong, noncommittal responses. She hadn't denied having a hand in the petition for Barker's stay of execution but she hadn't confirmed it, either. She'd explained with strength and conviction that she had only just learned she was, in fact, Olivia Barker. Her legal persona had taken over despite the circumstances and their state of dishevelment.

But this was only the beginning. As the news spread, all three women would be hunted down and revealed as the long-lost Barker children. There was no stopping this frenzy. Lyle McCaleb and Joel Hayden were on high alert for the wave to hit them by noon tomorrow. The Colby Agency would be bombarded with calls and protesters. This was going to get ugly.

Russ and Olivia were out in the open, where anyone could reach them. He held the curtain aside and checked the parking lot again. The only available parking was in the front, facing the street. He'd tucked the rental next door behind the pharmacy, which prevented it from being visible from the street. Problem was, this was the only motel in town and anyone looking for Olivia would start here. If they were lucky, most would assume they had left Granger.

Simon had no news on Clare and Weeden. No vehicles had been reported stolen from the area where the abandoned sedan they'd left behind had been found. No one matching their descriptions had taken public transportation or rented a vehicle from any agencies requiring ID. Depending on the funds readily available it was possible Weeden had purchased a used vehicle from an individual. The transaction wouldn't show up in the usual places so long as Weeden didn't attempt to register the vehicle and he wouldn't. With the news of Olivia's presence in Granger all over the airwaves, Weeden and Clare would be well aware of her movements.

Russ checked the weapon in his waistband and turned to consider the bathroom door. She'd announced she needed a long, hot soak as soon as they'd gotten into the room. She'd offered to let him shower first but he'd needed to confer with Simon so he'd passed.

She'd been in there a long time. As much as he didn't

want to disturb her, he needed to see that she was okay. He crossed the room and rapped on the door. "You doing all right in there?"

"I'd be doing a lot better if I were at a spa," she called out, her voice muffled by the closed door. "A good neck rubdown would be perfect right now."

He couldn't turn this into a spa but he'd been known to give a pretty damned good rubdown. His body tensed at the thought of touching her that way. Most likely it would be better if he stayed out here with that door between them. He'd already suffered a lapse in control when he'd permitted that kiss. As much as he understood allowing a personal connection to build, he couldn't regret kissing her.

"Take your time," he said, his voice sounding rusty. He cleared his throat. "Relax and those tense muscles will loosen up." Too bad he couldn't take his own advice. His whole body was rigid with tension that had everything to do with visions of her body.

He turned away from the door, proud of himself for doing the right thing, as challenging as that move was. "Good for you, pal," he muttered. This night was already going to be challenging enough with only one bed. The motel had one kind of room and those rooms had one bed. He wasn't about to let Olivia out of his sight, so sharing a room and a bed would have to work.

"Actually," she called out, "I was hoping you'd volunteer to give me a neck rub. I'm out of the tub now. Everything covered from neck to knee."

He closed his eyes. Wished she hadn't asked. The door opened and steam billowed out around him. A lungful of damp air filled his chest as the cloud dissipated and the image of Olivia, clad in only a towel, filled his eyes. Her hair was damp and clinging to her neck. Her skin was flushed from the warm soak and she looked as soft as smooth-whipped cream.

"I'm sorry." She sighed and ran her fingers through her hair. He tensed, worried or maybe hopeful that the towel would tumble to the floor. "I'm certain you want to have a shower and all I can think about is my own selfish pleasure."

"Trust me," he promised, the words sounding more like a growl, "skipping a shower to give you pleasure would not be a hardship."

Her eyes rounded as if she'd only just realized how her request sounded. "I'm sorry. I…" She shook her head. "I was about to say I didn't think of that, but the truth is that's all I thought about while I was relaxing in that steamy water."

She took the three steps that stood between them and stared up into his eyes. "I kept thinking about the way you kissed me and the idea that I've never enjoyed a kiss more. I'm certain it's the stress and the insanity circling around me right now. Desperation, too. Your kiss felt…real and fulfilling. Is that crazy or what?"

Considering he felt ready to tear off that towel and show her what true fulfillment was, he kept his mouth shut.

His silence did the trick. She stared at the well-worn carpet. "What am I doing? You're trying to do your job and I'm behaving like a teenage girl who doesn't understand the difference between physical attraction and the beginnings of a real bond between two people." She drew in a deep breath and met his eyes once more. "Forgive me, I'm not myself." She rolled her eyes. "With my track record, it's obvious I wouldn't know a real relationship if it hit me over the head with a gavel."

He couldn't let her dangle out there another second. "Relationships are complicated. I've bombed at a few myself."

"I can't even say that."

She went to the closet where he'd stowed their few belongings and rummaged through the bag from the store they'd hit last night. She pulled out a blouse and slacks and undies.

His throat went dry as he contemplated the idea that the tiny scrap of silk she held in her hand would soon be hugging that luscious bottom of hers.

"Turn around," she ordered.

Russ blinked. Tried to formulate a move based on her direction but it wasn't working.

She gave him an expectant look. "Turn around so I can get dressed. It's too humid in that bathroom. The fabric will just stick to my skin."

He turned around, his muscles screaming at the move. If he didn't get the need that she'd aroused under control soon he was going to explode.

"Guys tell me that I push them away." The sound of silk gliding across her skin whispered over his senses. "I've always thought they were just using that as an excuse to move on. But now—" the sound of a zipper skimming upward grated on his oversensitized nerves "—I wonder if maybe they were right. I think it's true. I don't know how to bond that way because of what happened when I was a child."

The closet door bumped to a close and he jumped. His brain kept assimilating images related to the sounds of her movements. He tightened his fingers into fists.

"Personally, I've always thought it was a cop-out when people blamed their issues on their childhoods. I mean, jeez, just because your mom or dad didn't show you any affection, did that mean you were destined to become an addict or serial killer?" The water came on in the sink, which was stationed outside the bathroom door. "Really, isn't our destiny our own to determine? We don't have to choose a certain path."

The swish and scrub of her brushing her teeth had him fighting the urge to turn around. Surely she was dressed by now, but she hadn't given him the okay. Should he just stand here like a statue and wonder?

More running water. More swishing and scrubbing, then

the inevitable whack of the toothbrush against the basin. "Guess I was wrong. I can see now that whatever happened in that house when I was a child has a direct correlation to my ability to trust and form bonds now. No matter how my adoptive parents tried, they couldn't erase the imprint of that horror."

She was opening up, trying to make sense of the emotional battle taking place inside her. He should be saying something. Offering his thoughts, cheering her on for coming to terms with her past…something…anything besides wishing he could strip those newly donned clothes off her and…

"There should be plenty of hot water by now." She touched his arm. He jerked, railed at himself for being so damned selfish. "You okay? You haven't said a word while I went on and on about my problems." She moved around in front of him and searched his face. "I really went off on a tangent, didn't I?" She bit her bottom lip. "Sorry about that. My boss and I carry on conversations like this all the time. It took years for me to feel comfortable having a discussion like this with him. He's probably my best friend as well as my boss. I've known you less than two days and already I feel comfortable."

The words were on the tip of his tongue. A nice, amiable response. A thank you for sharing and feeling able to do so. But none of that came out. "Why don't you take those clothes back off and let me show you just how comfortable things can get, the way I'm feeling right now." The ferocity in his tone startled even him. He wanted her badly…and he wanted her now.

She stared at him for three long seconds before her pupils flared with undeniable desire. "I…" She moistened those soft, pink lips. "I don't know what to say." She looked basically anywhere but at him.

He'd gone too far to back out now. "Don't say anything." His fingers were in her hair before he could stop himself.

Her breath caught as he closed his mouth over hers. The sweet minty taste filled him and he wanted to taste every square inch of her. Her fingers were tearing at the buttons of his shirt. His were fumbling with the hem of her blouse. They worked around each other, the moves seemingly choreographed as her blouse came over her head and off and his shirt was peeled away from his back and arms.

The idea that he should have taken that shower flitted through his head but he couldn't slow down long enough to ponder the notion—not when she wore no bra and her firm, high breasts were right in front of him, the nipples hard with need. His palms closed over the lush mounds and she leaned into his touch. He lowered his head and tasted first one then the other before ushering her down onto the bed. He lowered her zipper and dragged off her slacks, leaving nothing but that scrap of black silk covering her hips.

Russ stood at the foot of the bed and admired her body for a moment. She was trim and athletic with just enough feminine curves to add up to pure perfection. He unfastened his belt, liking that she watched his every move. He placed his weapon on the bed and tugged off his jeans. The condom in his wallet went down next to the weapon. Then he hauled off his stained jeans and tossed them aside. His shorts went next.

She continued to openly study him and he liked it. His body hardened even more as her gaze roved over his lower anatomy. He shucked his socks and reached for the condom. The pulse at the base of her throat fluttered as he watched her watching him tear open the necessary precaution. He skimmed the protection over his arousal and moved onto the bed, crawling on all fours up the length of her.

Belatedly, he grabbed the weapon and put it on the bedside table and reached for the light.

"Leave it on."

Surprised that she wanted the light on, he lowered his

hand back to the bed. In his experience women most often wanted the light off.

"I like looking at you." She reached up and feathered her fingers down his chest. "Your body is amazing. So strong." She stroked his chest again, only this time her hands moved even lower, allowing her fingertips to glide over his length. "You make me want to do things I've never even considered before."

He lowered his face closer to hers. "We'll do whatever you want, Liv." He brushed his lips across hers. "Just tell me what it is you want most and we'll start there." His body was vibrating with the urge to take her hard and fast but he wanted to do this right. To make her feel all those wondrous sensations she'd missed out on before.

She encircled his arousal with her fingers. "I want this now." As if to underscore her demand, she wrapped her legs around his and lifted her hips.

As much as he wanted to grant her every wish, he needed to be sure she was ready. Reaching downward, he trailed a finger down her abdomen, traced those most intimate parts of her and then delved inside. She was ready all right. Hot, slick and undulating invitingly against his touch.

He shifted to his knees and lifted her bottom with one hand while guiding himself into her with the other. Once he was inside her just far enough, he grasped her hips with both hands and held her steady as he slowly thrust fully inside her.

Her fingers fisted in the sheets as her body rose instinctively to meet him. Her cries told him she wanted more so he began to move, ensuring full penetration with each drive of his hips. She climaxed almost instantly. That only fueled the fire roaring inside him. Made him want to bring her to that place over and over again before he plunged over that incredible edge.

To do that he had to slow things down. He started with

her nose, kissing her face…all those features he adored. The dimples that appeared when she smiled, like now. Those long, long lashes that shaded her big dark eyes. Her chin…that long slender neck. And those breasts, man he loved her breasts. Just the right size. He moved down her slender rib cage, paid special attention to her belly button and then he showed her how a man could cherish a woman's most intimate places.

When she screamed with release a second time, it was his turn. He filled her over and over, until she came with him. Then he slumped onto the bed and drew her into his arms. If not for needing a shower so bad, he could have snuggled that way right there for the rest of the night.

He waited until she was sleeping soundly before slipping away. With his weapon in hand, he stalked to the bathroom and climbed into the shower. Leaving the door open to the room and working as quickly as possible, he was in and out of the shower in about three minutes. He tugged on clean jeans and a tee. He had more socks but he'd either have to do laundry or make another hit on a department store for shorts. Didn't matter. The well-worn jeans suited him just fine.

To his surprise, Olivia was not only awake but dressed and sitting on the side of the bed when he came out of the bathroom. He joined her and waited for her to say what was on her mind. He hoped she wasn't already regretting their lovemaking.

Without meeting his gaze, she asked, "Should we talk about this?" She shrugged. "I don't usually get intimate with strangers."

And there came the guilt. He reached over and took her by the chin to turn her face to his. "We've shared too much the last thirty-six hours to be called strangers. What people feel is not always best measured in terms of time. At this moment we need each other and maybe that need won't be as intense tomorrow or the next day but that doesn't change what it is right now."

Her lips trembled into a smile. "Have you ever considered changing career paths? You'd make a very persuasive trial attorney."

"I'm not sure that's a compliment, but I'll take it as one coming from you."

A solid rap on the door had him reaching for the weapon at the small of his back. "Go in the bathroom and shut the door."

He got another surprise when she actually did as he said without a word in challenge.

Russ went to the side of the window farthest from the door and lifted the curtain away just far enough to get a look at the person knocking. The light at the door revealed a man in a rumpled suit. As the guy reached up to knock again, he set his left hand on his hip, pushing his suit jacket aside as he did so. The weapon and badge attached to his belt shouted *cop* loud and clear.

Russ noted only one sedan in the dimly lit parking lot besides the two that had been there when they arrived. Obviously the guy was alone.

The two deputies who had showed up at the old Barker place had apparently informed the detectives division. Judging by the guy's age he was old enough to have worked the Princess Killer case. Gray hair, glasses, lean, wiry frame for a man undoubtedly well into sixty. Time to find out.

Russ tucked his own weapon back into his waistband, in front so the guy could see it, and then reached for the door. When he and the man with the badge stood face-to-face, Russ waited for him to speak first.

"Detective Marcus Whitt," he said without offering any other ID as proof of his word. "Mr. St. James, may I have a few minutes of your time?"

"Sure." Russ stepped back and opened the door wider, then

closed it behind the detective. "Have a seat." There were two chairs flanking a small table in front of the window.

"That's not necessary." The detective braced his hands on his hips and got right to the point. "Ms. Westfield came to see me last week and I told her in no uncertain terms that there was nothing to be gained by digging around in the Barker case. Apparently that message didn't get through to her. I don't know how much you know about this case, but your agency has a reputation for doing the right thing. I'm certainly hoping you'll do the right thing here and take Ms. Westfield home before this gets any worse. She's already caused enough pain to the families of the victims by pursuing a stay of execution for that monster Rafe Barker."

Russ weighed his words for a bit, mostly to keep him calm. The man was more than a little worked up. "I appreciate you stopping by, Detective, but you need to be aware that I work for Ms. Westfield. If she wants to look into the case, then that's what we'll do."

"I'll be calling your superior," Whitt threatened. "One travesty of the justice system has already taken place with the overturning of Clare Barker's sentence. I'm not going to sit back and wait while another killer gets off."

"What is it you plan to do? It's a free country as long as no laws are broken. It's not like we blew up anyone's car or slashed their tires."

"Are you accusing me of something, St. James?" He cocked his head. "I'm not a P.I. like you. I have a sworn duty to uphold the law. The citizens of Granger depend on people like me to ensure the bad guys are taken off the streets and *kept* off the streets. It's people like you and that misguided woman you're with who hurt those who've already been hurt far too much."

"Misguided?" Olivia joined their friendly meeting. "That's what you think I am? Rafe and Clare Barker were charged with numerous murders, including the murders of their three daughters. Clearly mistakes were made. If one or both are guilty, then they deserve the sentence levied by the courts. But the fact that my sisters and I are alive insists that we take a second look. You should be the first in line to ensure that it's done properly."

"The investigation was conducted properly the first time," he argued with fury vibrating in his voice. "Your father murdered those girls. I don't know why or how you and your sisters were spared, thank God you were, but I know what that monster did. I helped bring those remains out of those woods. I know what they did."

"We understand your position," Russ stepped in. "That's why we've been trying to conduct our investigation as discreetly as possible. I don't know who tipped the media off to our presence but this kind of attention was not our intent. My agency felt and still feels that Ms. Westfield and her sisters may be in danger from Tony Weeden and perhaps even Clare Barker. We're doing all we can to keep them out of the media's keen focus."

Whitt looked from Russ to Olivia and back. "I guess we'll just have to agree to disagree on the matter."

"We could work together," Olivia offered. "Go over the details of the case and see if looking back twenty years later we see something that was missed in the heat of emotion. That case was a nightmare for all involved. It would've been easy to overlook something small or to see something the wrong way through that lens of so many volatile emotions."

Whitt's lips formed a grim line and Russ felt certain he was going to blast Olivia for suggesting he'd made a mistake. "All right. Let's do that. If you think you can see something I missed, let's have at it. Then you'll know what I knew back then—that Rafe and Clare Barker are cold-blooded killers."

Olivia squared her shoulders. "I'm ready right now."

Except for her shoes, Russ thought. They were both standing there with bare feet.

"Follow me to my office and I'll show you everything."

Chapter Fifteen

Wednesday, June 5th, 3:45 a.m.

Olivia could hardly stay focused on one single aspect of the case Detective Whitt had laid out on the conference table. The crime scene photos were sickening and there were far more than Keisha Landers had had in her possession. The descriptions of the conditions in the home and clinic were deplorable. What had happened those last few months? The vague memories that had surfaced showed a clean, if not modern, home. Mrs. Samson had said the same. But then it all went downhill afterward.

"We couldn't determine the full extent of the atrocities the girls suffered from their remains," Whitt said. "We would know more now but twenty-some years ago we worked with what we had. The bodies were dismembered and placed in wooden boxes." He pointed to one of the photos. "Then buried in that makeshift graveyard they used for the animals they couldn't save. Back before the arrests, the Barkers had a regular pet cemetery going back there. Folks would bring their deceased pets and Rafe would show them a spot they could use."

"There were four other girls who went missing that you suspected were connected to the Princess Killer case," Olivia noted.

"Four for certain but we suspect there were six or more, but we couldn't connect those with any real certainty. The remains we found were of girls all pictured on Rafe's pet-adoption bulletin board he kept in the clinic. Those victims had been missing for years. Every parent of a missing daughter remembered the seemingly kind veterinarian referring to their daughter as a princess when they visited the clinic. But it was the final victims before he was caught that we never found. Four for sure, maybe more. Those girls went missing very close together, which was a different MO from the previous abductions. With the others it was one a year, then suddenly four or more go missing in the space of as many months. We think that's when he started to unravel and his house of horrors fell in on him, so to speak."

"You were part of a fairly large task force," Russ put in. He'd spent most of the past hour listening. Olivia had spent that same time avoiding eye contact with him. As much as she wanted to be cool with what happened in the motel room, a part of her was mortified at her uncharacteristic boldness with him. She generally reserved that side of her personality for work.

"I was lead, but I worked with four other detectives from surrounding counties and two FBI agents." To Olivia he added, "We made no mistakes. The evidence we used to determine that the three of you had fallen prey to foul play was perhaps minimal but we had every reason to believe you were gone. Clare was hysterical. She kept saying over and over that he had killed her babies."

He surveyed the stacks of interview reports and crime scene reports and shook his head. "Maybe we should have dug further but we had no compelling reason to." He fixed his weary gaze on Olivia. "Looking back, I can say without reservation that you were better off being whisked away from that nightmare. The investigation took weeks and weeks. The trial went on for months and months. It was a legal and moral nightmare for all involved. For the families of the victims and the rest of the community, it was an unparalleled tragedy. The whole town was in mourning."

Olivia couldn't deny he had a valid point but that didn't change what she needed to know. "One of the witnesses you interviewed has told us that there was another woman present in the Barker home for quite some time before the arrests." Olivia didn't want to mention Mrs. Samson's name. "Did anything your investigation discovered suggest there was a third adult in the house?"

"Mrs. Samson, yes." Whitt picked up his third cup of coffee and had a swallow, then grimaced. "She mentioned seeing another woman, who bore a striking resemblance to Clare. But Clare denied another woman's presence. Since she had no living relatives that we could find, we assumed Mrs. Samson was mistaken. The other witness," he hastened to add before Olivia could point it out, "only saw this other woman once and wasn't really sure it wasn't Clare. We found no prints that pointed to anyone else. Of course, our print databases weren't what they are now."

"There was a murder in Copperas Cove a couple of weeks ago," Russ said. "A woman, Janet Tolliver. Is it possible to check any prints you have on file from the Barker home during your investigation to the ones discovered in this recent investigation? Specifically to those of Tolliver?"

"It would take some time." Whitt shrugged. "But if you think it's important I could get it done. Who is this Tolliver woman and how does she connect to the Barkers?"

"She was Clare's sister. She and Clare were separated when Clare was only three, we believe, because Janet had violent tendencies. Later, as adults, the two reconnected and Janet was the one keeping Rafe's secrets about his daughters. She could be the other blonde woman who looked so much like

Clare. And if she was there, you can bet she had a hand in whatever atrocities were taking place."

Olivia's heart bumped her sternum. How would she have gotten this far without Russ? He'd elbowed his way into her life and now she couldn't imagine going through this without him. How would she handle him walking away when his job was done? She suddenly felt completely alone. Her biological parents were killers, or at the very least completely mental. She had damaged her relationship with her family and latched onto a man whose sole purpose was to serve as her protector.

How screwed up was that?

She shook off the painful thoughts and focused on the discussion she'd wanted so desperately to have with this detective. She'd felt certain he was holding something back when in reality he had not. He and the others had done the best they could with what they had. The evidence, though not directly connected to Clare, had been damning. Had Olivia been involved with the case, as she saw it spread out before her right now, she couldn't say that she would have done anything any differently.

Not a single thing.

"Excuse me." Detective Whitt reached for his ringing cell phone and stepped away from the conference table.

"How're you feeling about this?" Russ asked quietly.

She surveyed the mountain of paperwork. "I feel they did everything possible. I was wrong to blame the authorities involved with investigating this case." Her gaze sought his. "Whatever discrepancies…whatever the truth really is…it lies with Rafe and Clare. Janet's dead so she can't tell us anything." Olivia took a breath and said what she knew needed to be on the table with the rest of this monstrosity of a puzzle. "I believe the only way we'll ever get anything else is from Clare. If she survives her partnership with Weeden."

Clare, whether she was innocent of those long-ago crimes

or not, was in danger now. Olivia felt it all the way to the core of her being. Somehow, though he had likely killed her, Weeden had been involved with Janet in recent years. And Janet had no doubt been involved with Rafe. Was it possible that Clare had been an innocent victim? Maybe with a few loose screws? Taking into account her crazy family, that last part was a given.

"I can't let you take a chance like that. Trying to connect with Clare is too dangerous." Russ shook his head firmly from side to side. "Whatever you believe could be gained, it's not worth the risk to your safety. If she would willingly come forward, under the right circumstances, then no problem. But not on the sly. No way."

Olivia crossed her arms over her chest. "You do realize I'm a grown woman," she countered.

He reached out, stroked her cheek with the pad of his thumb. She shivered. "Unconditionally."

"Then—" she cleared her throat of the emotion that tightened it "—you understand I can make that decision without your permission or your approval."

"You can," he agreed, "but you understand that I'm a hell of a lot stronger than you and I will do whatever it takes to protect you from all danger, including any your own decisions pose." He held up a hand to silence her when she would have launched her next objection. "And that part has nothing to do with the job. It's about you and me."

Her heart stumbled and the words she wanted to say wouldn't form on her tongue.

He gifted her with the dazzling smile that took her breath away every single time. "I like it when you're speechless."

"There's someone here who wants to see the two of you if you're willing," Detective Whitt announced.

Olivia whirled to face him. "Clare?" Would she turn herself in like this? "Is Weeden with her?"

"It's not Clare. It's Claude Henson. He's the father of one of the girls who was buried on the Barker farm. He has something to say to you about what happened to your SUV."

Whitt led the way to an interview room where an older man sat at a table with another detective. He reminded Olivia of her adoptive father. She recognized the weary lines that warned he'd worried himself sick about whatever he had to say. In Olivia's case, her father was usually worried about something she had done or planned to do.

"Mr. Henson, this is Olivia Westfield and her friend Mr. St. James," Whitt said, making the introductions.

Henson and the other detective stood. Henson shook his head and stared a moment at the cup of coffee he held in his hand. "I was the one who slashed the tires on your vehicle." He lifted his gaze to Olivia. "A friend of mine over in Livingston called and said he'd heard from a reporter with inside information what you were up to. The petition for a stay of execution and all. He said that his source mentioned you were coming here to look into the investigation." He shrugged. "I drove all over town until I found an outsider's vehicle. Since it was parked at that awful place, I knew it was you." He heaved a burdened breath. "I was wrong. I'll pay for the damages if you'll allow me to." He glanced at the detective who'd been speaking to him. "And I'll face whatever charges are appropriate."

Olivia found her voice. "Sir, you don't owe me an apology. I can't imagine how you suffered at the hands of one or both of the people who are unfortunately my biological parents. I'm the one who owes you an apology." She turned to Whitt. "I owe you one, as well. I came here last week all fired up to prove you hadn't done your job. I convinced myself that because my sisters and I are alive that perhaps my parents weren't the monsters you had painted them to be.

But I was wrong to come with that attitude. All I want is the truth. Whatever that is."

Russ pressed his hand to her back and she'd never needed that kind of support more. The mere touch told her he was not only beside her, he was with her on this.

"I have no desire to press charges," Russ added. "I mentioned that last night when the report was written. My insurance will pay for the damages. Let's leave it at that."

"I guess you can go, Mr. Henson," the other detective offered. To Russ he said, "That's very obliging of you."

Russ gave him an acknowledging nod.

Mr. Henson paused at the door and turned to Olivia. "You look a lot like your mother. She brought you and your sisters to church every Sunday long after Rafe stopped coming. I guess if I'd been the kind of Christian I should have been I would have known something was wrong then. And when she stopped coming at all, every one of us should have noticed and acted. But we let it go. I've had to live with that mistake for more than twenty years. I don't care to live with it anymore."

Olivia touched his arm and managed a faint smile. "Thank you, Mr. Henson. If we learn anything new about what happened we'll be sure to see that Detective Whitt lets you know."

He gave her a nod and went on his way.

Half an hour later Russ had parked the rented sedan behind the pharmacy next door to the Boxcar Motel. Olivia was beyond exhausted. She desperately needed sleep. Without nightmares hopefully.

When Russ was satisfied that the coast was clear he led her to the door of their room. Dawn was peeking through the darkness. It would be daylight soon…barely two more weeks until Rafe's execution. Part of her wanted him to die. He had to have committed those awful kidnappings and murders. But what if she was wrong? What if it had been Clare?

"Hold on."

Russ drew her back when she was only three or four steps from the door. She started to ask why and then she saw the package on the sidewalk in front of their door. Mostly it looked like wadded-up newspaper.

"I want you to move back and get behind that truck on the other side of the parking lot."

"Shouldn't you call Detective Whitt? Nine-one-one or someone?" The concept that it could be another bomb had fear throttling at full speed through her veins.

"I'm going to have a look and see what we have here. Now go," he ordered.

Olivia hurried across the lot and got behind the truck she presumed belonged to the manager or motel owner. She held her breath as Russ approached the door and leaned down to gingerly inspect the clump of newspapers.

When he reached inside she almost cried out his name. And he was always lecturing her about risks.

He studied the object he'd removed for a moment. She tried to make out what it was but she was too far away. A small box of some sort. He opened it and inspected the inside, then closed it again.

"It's okay. It's a music box." He motioned for her to join him.

She hurried over, curious to see the object up close. "A music box?"

He twisted the key on the bottom and opened the lid so the tune would play.

Olivia froze.

That was the tune. The humming she heard in her nightmares. The tune her mother used to hum whenever she was rocking the baby...Sadie.

"That's my mother's music box." The words were hardly more than a whisper. "She knows we're here. She's been here."

7:30 a.m.

RUSS HADN'T SLEPT MORE than a few seconds in the past hour. He scrubbed a hand across his face and considered the newspaper he had smoothed out from the crumpled mess that had been wrapped around the music box.

The stick-figure drawing was the same one Clare had been leaving in her wake. Only this time it was only the mother figure, the three girls and then a small boy figure that represented Laney's son. Tony Weeden was not a part of this drawing as he had been in the ones she had left behind in Beaumont. In the ones that had included Weeden, his figure had been drawn larger than the three girls.

Did that mean she and Weeden were about to have a parting of ways? From what he knew about Weeden, Russ wasn't sure Clare would come out the victor from a battle with her son. Since the stick figures in this drawing hadn't been crossed out with big X's as the ones had in the motel room in Beaumont that Lucas discovered when he suspected Clare and Weeden were watching Laney, did that mean she and Weeden had already parted ways? One thing was certain, she was here in Granger. With Weeden's and her faces all over the news, she was taking a hell of a chance coming here. This was the last place she would want to be captured even if for nothing more than questioning.

What was the point in sending this music box? Olivia had said that she had heard the tune in her nightmares. Was Clare hoping to trigger more memories? Was she that certain that what Olivia would remember would prove to all with doubts that she was innocent?

Once they entered their motel room, Russ made a call to Simon to update him on the tire slasher and the delivery of the music box. Rafe Barker still refused to speak to anyone from the Colby Agency. Simon suspected that he had called

Victoria to the prison at precisely the time that would cause her to be caught up in the protesters and the media frenzy. Like Russ, all at the Colby Agency suspected Rafe was using them for an agenda that was nothing like the one he had presented to Victoria in his letter or at their first meeting.

Detective Whitt would call as soon as he had anything on those prints. It would take some time since twenty-two years ago collection and storage of evidence had been done a little differently. Russ wasn't sure what they would accomplish by confirming Janet Tolliver's presence in the Barker home without Clare to explain what that meant, but it was a detail they hadn't known until now. It was impossible to know which tiny seemingly insignificant detail would matter.

He shifted in the chair to watch Olivia sleep. He hadn't meant to get this deeply entangled, particularly not with a client. But he was squarely there and there was no turning back now. When this was over, they had things to sort out. He wasn't simply going away.

The midst of a stressful and desperate investigation like this was the least desirable launching point for a prospective relationship, but sometimes life sneaked up on a guy like that. He wanted to explore these feelings. Maybe that made him soft, but it was the truth. He'd always found that living by the truth and one's honor was the best way. At thirty-five he wasn't about to change that now.

His lips slid into a smile. He enjoyed watching her like this, all soft and vulnerable. The idea that this woman trusted him enough to sleep under his watch shifted something in his chest. She was no pushover. Definitely no shrinking violet. Gaining her trust and her respect was a big deal and he savored the idea that he had earned that from her. Particularly in such a short time.

She damn sure had earned his respect and trust. He'd never met a woman any stronger. Except maybe Victoria. And his mother. She was a strong woman, as well. The thought of introducing Olivia to his mother had another of those strange little curls of emotion happening in his chest. He hadn't been in love before so he couldn't hazard a guess as to whether this was it or not, but he knew for sure that whatever it was, he wanted it to last.

The urge to climb into that bed with Olivia and make love again was powerful. But she needed sleep and he was fresh out of condoms. He carried one in his wallet at all times. Not that he planned casual sex but it was better to be safe than sorry.

Her respiration grew rapid and uneven and the pained look on her face had him moving to the side of the bed. No sooner than he settled in next to her she started to flail and cry out.

She was having another nightmare. Dammit.

"Olivia." He took her by the shoulders and shook her gently.

She tried to twist out of his hold, tried to fight him off. "Olivia, wake up."

Her eyes flew open and she screamed.

"Olivia, it's me, darling. It's okay. You were dreaming."

She blinked, inhaled a ragged breath. "Oh, God."

Before he could try and calm her she scrambled away from him and off the other side of the bed. A smile tugged at his lips just watching her pace the room wearing nothing but his shirt. Man, she was gorgeous.

"It was her." She turned to him, her body trembling. "Janet. It was her."

He stood and moved toward her. "What do you mean it was her?"

"She was at the house during those final days or weeks." Olivia nodded frantically. "And she was up to something."

"What did you remember exactly?"

"I woke up from a bad dream and I went in search of my

mother." She moistened her lips. "Only when I went into her room it wasn't her in the bed with my father. It was Janet."

Olivia hugged her arms around her middle. "That's why I felt repulsed by the thought of going into their room when we were at the house."

Russ went to her and put his arms around her.

She stared up at him. "Bad things happened there, Russ. Things we don't even know yet."

Chapter Sixteen

8:00 a.m.

Clare had made her decision. No matter what Tony said she was going to see her daughters. All she had to do was get them all to meet her somewhere. Anywhere. The only way she imagined she would be able to do that was to call that woman...the head of the Colby Agency.

Tony would be angry. She glanced at him still covered head to toe in the bed. His gunshot wound was infected. He knew this and still he refused to go to a doctor. Though he was a nurse and he was on the antibiotics he had taken from that clinic, there was a problem.

She had wanted to believe in her son. He was so smart and he had done so well for himself. She had prayed for him over the years. But Janet and those awful people who had adopted him had ruined him.

Clare feared there was no hope for his redemption.

She hadn't driven in more than twenty years when she'd had to race away from her old house with Tony bleeding like a stuck pig. That had proved that driving was like riding a bicycle. One never forgot how.

Maybe she should just slip out while he slept. They had hurried away from Granger after delivering the package to the motel where Olivia was staying. They'd gotten to this

small town before Tony had complained that he was too tired
to go on. He'd taken some of the pain pills he'd stolen from
the clinic, as well, so he might not wake up for a while yet.
That would prevent an ugly confrontation. She didn't want
to leave him on bad terms. Whatever he had become in his
life it was her fault in large part.

God had blessed her with a child after that awful rape.
She should have kept her child and faced the consequences
like a grown-up. Instead, she'd run to the only family she'd
had left. Janet had given her bad advice. She had used the
opportunity to hurt Clare yet again. Worse she had hurt an
innocent child. She had ruined his life.

Perhaps Clare shouldn't leave him. She could try harder
to make him see right from wrong. When this mess was all
cleared up maybe they could join a small church and let God
cleanse them. And she would have the chance to make up for
her terrible mistakes. Tony deserved more from her.

But she had begun to worry that he might hold a grudge
in his heart against the girls. Clare could not let him hurt the
girls. Like him, they had suffered enough already.

She peeked beyond the curtain and checked the parking
lot. It was cracked and weeds had long ago grown up in those
cracks. The building was surely on its way to being con-
demned. But that had made it safe for them.

Only two other cars were in the lot. Old, beat-up cars like
the one Tony had purchased from a man with two cars for
sale in his front yard. Tony had plenty of money. He would
be all right without her. Once this trouble was cleared up he
could get another nursing job and all would be well for him.
He'd said he didn't kill that man. Surely the police would
find the truth.

Like they found it twenty-two years ago?

Clare shuddered. That had been different. There were
things she couldn't tell the police. Things that would have

made the difference, but her hands had been tied. All she could do was try to convince them that she was innocent and pray that justice would prevail.

But it had not…not for more than twenty years.

Clare dismissed those haunting memories and painful emotions. She couldn't change the past. She had to focus on the here and now. If her being a part of Tony's life was going to cause him pain, perhaps leaving was the right thing to do. But she hated to go without telling him she loved him and appreciated all that he had done. Well, most all that he had done. Some things she wasn't so sure about but she was only human.

She would leave him a note. Then she would drive to Houston and demand to see this Victoria Colby-Camp. As a mother herself, surely she would understand Clare's position.

Clare took her time emptying the paper sack of food supplies she'd gotten from the grocery store. The motel had no writing paper but there was the pen she had used when she'd left that note for Olivia. Well, it hadn't really been a note. More an omen. Even then she had known that this moment was coming. It was time for her to stand on her own and stop depending on her son to take care of her.

She flattened the bag and carefully wrote a note to her son. Taking care to say all the right things, she told him how much she loved him and how sorry she was for not taking care of him as a mother should have. He had deserved better and she had failed him. She hoped he would one day forgive her. She told him of her plan to go to see the woman at the Colby Agency. Clare had as good a chance of swaying her as Rafe had had. Better maybe since they were both women and mothers. Tears welled in her eyes as she told Tony how she wanted to be reunited with her daughters and that this was the only way. When this was over perhaps they could all be together. She signed it with much love and then drew a little heart.

With the note left where he would see it first thing when he woke up, Clare gathered her few items. A change of clothes and a hairbrush. She didn't need anything else. There was a bus station not far from here. The car was Tony's and it would be wrong for her to take it.

She had a small amount of cash of her own. They'd given it to her along with her few earthly possessions when she left the prison. Surely two hundred dollars would be adequate to get her from here to Houston.

Moving quietly, she eased toward the door. Once she reached it she had to carefully remove the security chain and then pray he wouldn't hear the knob turn.

"Where do you think you're going?"

Clare froze. Think! She needed an excuse. "I thought I would go out and get us some breakfast." She pasted a smile on her face and turned around. Her lips dragged into a frown. He held that awful gun aimed right at her.

"Is that right?" He threw back the covers and sat up. "Is that why you're carrying that stuff?"

Fear pumped through her veins. "I was…was going to put them in the car so I wouldn't forget about them. They're all I have."

He snatched the keys up from the bedside table. "Really? How did you plan to unlock the car? I keep it locked, you know."

"I forgot. Silly me." She pushed her smile back into place. "Would you like some breakfast?" His T-shirt was bloody. The wound was bleeding again.

"Sit down over there." He waved the gun toward the chair.

Her body trembling so much she wasn't sure she would be able to walk, she pointed herself in the direction of the chair and moved toward it. "I'm very hungry this morning." Please, please let him believe her.

He got up and started toward the bathroom.

If he went into the bathroom she could still get away without him catching her.

He stopped at the console where the broken television sat and reached down.

Her heart lurched wildly as he picked up the paper sack she'd written the note on.

The seconds ticking past screamed in her ears. Finally, he turned around slowly and aimed the gun at her once more. "Love you, too, Mommy."

Chapter Seventeen

Bay Point, 9:30 a.m.

Victoria sat down on the chair facing the sofa. Her husband was the most stubborn man she had ever met. He absolutely would not listen to reason.

"We have to come to some sort of agreement, Lucas," she argued yet again. "I will not have you taking these kinds of risks anymore. It's far too dangerous."

It pained her to look at the awful bandage on his forehead and the walking cast on his good leg. Dear God, what else did it take for him to see that they were too old for this business? Enough was enough. The Colby Agency was in good hands. Let the next generation take the reins.

Lucas closed the novel he'd been reading and set it aside. He removed the eyeglasses that he never allowed anyone save Victoria to see and put them aside, as well. "We can come to an agreement right now but it would be a wasted effort."

"You're wrong this time, Lucas." She squared her shoulders and lifted her chin in defiance of the little voice his words awakened. "I will not change my mind. We are officially retiring. No more cases. None."

"And what will you do the next time you receive a letter from a desperate client? Or a call from someone in need?"

The man knew her too well. "I won't be receiving any letters or calls because no one, outside of our family and Simon and Ian, will know this address or this number." She intended to do this thing this time. It was well past time they stopped kidding themselves. They should be traveling and enjoying life, not working cases that put them in the line of fire.

He made a harrumphing sound. "All right. Where are we off to first? A cruise? A trip to Europe? Name the place and we'll go. Just leave all the business cares behind and fly off into the sunset."

"We'll need to wait until you're fully recovered first. Then we'll make a list of all the places we've always wanted to visit. We'll prioritize them and start checking off destinations." She smiled, feeling good about making this decision once and for all.

"In the meantime I suppose we can oversee all that redecorating you want to do."

That he made the task sound less than palatable grated on her nerves. Did he truly not want to retire? Had that knock on the head rattled him to the point that he was confused? They'd had this conversation months ago and he'd been all for retirement.

"Don't make it sound like such a dreaded chore. Do you not want to redecorate?" It wasn't absolutely necessary. If he was opposed, that was certainly all right with her.

He patted the sofa next to him. "Come over here and sit by me, my love."

With a dramatic display of reluctance she did as he asked. Once she was seated he put his arm around her and hugged her close. "Victoria, I love you more than you can possibly fathom. As I know you love me."

She rested her head on his strong shoulder. "Then why won't you see reason on this? We've had a wonderful three decades. It's time to move on to that next stage in our lives, like normal people do."

He laughed, the sound rumbling up from his chest. "My dear, we have never been and we will never be normal. Surely you recognize that. There are people who rescue and there are those who get rescued. We're the rescuers. The world needs us."

"We need us." She rose up and looked him in the eye. "I need you."

"Now we get to the true heart of the matter. You're afraid. Not for yourself, but for me."

It was true. She couldn't deny it. "Yes. I want us to take the time we never seemed to have in the past and enjoy each other. We discussed this all before and you agreed that it was the best decision."

"And then you answered Rafe Barker's call to come see him in prison and you were bombarded and harassed by protesters and reporters. It did little good for me to agree if you aren't going to abide by that mutual agreement."

The situation cleared for her. This wasn't about him having second thoughts. This was about him being worried about *her*.

"I'm finished with that case," Victoria proclaimed. "Simon and his staff have it under control. There is nothing else I can do. I'm done, Lucas. I want to begin plans for our first trip."

Her desperation was showing and that was never attractive. The memory of hearing that he had been found in that ravine, half-dead, still haunted her. She couldn't face the possibility of another call like that.

"Very well. You've convinced me." He pressed a kiss to her cheek. "What city is at the top of your list, Victoria? Where in the world would you go first?"

The telephone rang and she sighed. "Hold that thought." Satisfied that she and Lucas were on the same page now, she went in search of the house phone. She checked the screen. The office.

"Hello, Simon, how are you this morning?" This would

be as good a time as any to let him know that she was off the case.

"Victoria, we have a situation."

The seriousness of his tone warned that it was not a good situation. "What's going on?" From the corner of her eye she saw Lucas's eyebrows rear up.

"It's Clare Barker. She just called here and she wants a meeting with you. Today, Victoria. She wants to meet with you today. She says she's ready to give you the whole story on what really happened twenty-two years ago. But she will only give it to you and her daughters. She will not negotiate those conditions."

The certainty that she was finished with this case, that Simon and the others had everything under control, vanished. There was no other option.

"Tell her I'll be there."

Chapter Eighteen

Barker Farm, Granger, 3:30 p.m.

Olivia sat perfectly still for a long moment after Russ parked the SUV. The others were already here. The meeting with Clare wasn't until four o'clock, but Victoria Colby-Camp wanted time for the introductions and for preparation.

Russ, along with the other two Colby investigators who had been protecting the Barker offspring, would have to leave before that time. Part of the conditions of the meet was that all three bodyguards were to stay clear of the old farmhouse.

"You holding up okay?"

Olivia turned to Russ. "It helps that you're here." Just the sound of his voice made her feel safe and strong.

"You know we have backup in position already. Two of my colleagues, including Simon Ruhl, are in the house along with two of Detective Whitt's men. There's a whole army of cops in the woods. They've been there for hours just in case Weeden has been watching this afternoon."

"Clare said she would be alone."

"She won't be alone. She may appear alone, but he'll be here somewhere. You can count on it."

Olivia resisted the urge to twist in her seat to scan the area. She tried to steady herself. Her entire being seemed to quake with uncertainty. "On some level I've wanted this reunion of sorts since the moment I learned I was adopted. But it's a big risk to all of us, isn't it?"

"It is. We don't know what either or both have planned but we're assuming the worst."

"I guess I'll see you later, then." Regret washed over her at the idea that this might be the last time she saw him. If she died today—or if he did—they would never know what might have been. For that she was immensely sorry. She had called her parents and apologized for blaming them in any way for trying to protect her from the past. It didn't excuse what she had done or make up for it but at least the air between them had been cleared.

Russ nodded. "I'll be waiting."

Somehow her lips stretched into a smile. Maybe it was the certainty in his eyes and his voice. He had no intention of losing her to Weeden or Clare or anyone else. Her heart filled to overflowing.

"I'm holding you to that promise, cowboy."

He leaned across the console and kissed her. Not a demanding kiss, just a simple, sweet, more-to-come kind of kiss. When he drew back she had to go. Another second and she'd never be able to walk away from him.

He waited until she had reached the door. It opened and Victoria Colby-Camp waited in the entry hall for her. Olivia didn't look back. Watching Russ drive away was more than she could handle right now. She entered the house that held the secrets of her nightmares.

Olivia had not met Victoria, but she had seen her face in the news and Russ had told her how courageous and strong Victoria was. That she was willing to be here for this meeting, at such great risk to herself, spoke volumes.

"Olivia, I'm so pleased to finally meet you. Your sisters are waiting in the parlor."

Olivia fixed a smile in place. "Thank you." Her heart was

racing and her hands were shaking so she clasped them behind her back as she followed the head of the Colby Agency into the parlor room on the left.

Laney and Sadie stood in the center of the room, both looking about as nervous as she did. Laney was taller with hair the color of Olivia's only much longer. Her eyes were the same rich brown. Sadie was more petite, tiny almost. Her hair was a lighter blond, like Clare's had once been, and she had the green eyes of their mother. Both her sisters wore their usual cowgirl duds, boots included. They were beautiful. Pride tightened her chest.

Olivia wondered what they thought of her. She felt a little overdressed in her skirt and blouse. She'd had to buy something to wear today. Maybe she should have bought jeans. But this was who she was, no need to try and conceal that. They were all three grown women now with different ways and thoughts on life. They were strangers, really. An ache twisted in her heart. No matter what happened today, Olivia hoped this was the first step toward changing that sad reality.

"Olivia Westfield," Victoria announced, "this is Laney Seagers and Sadie Gilmore. Your sisters."

Olivia tried to smile but her trembling lips wouldn't hold the expression. "Hello. I'm glad we're finally together again."

Her sisters stared at her without speaking or smiling or anything at all. Olivia's heart rammed harder and harder against her chest. The urge to apologize for not protecting them came out of nowhere and had her eyes burning like fire.

Suddenly the two were surrounding her, hugging her and kissing her cheeks. Olivia couldn't help herself. She cried like a baby. The tears and hugs went on and on until they were all three emotionally exhausted. And then they simply stood there in a circle, holding hands and staring at each other.

"You always took care of us," Laney said. She pressed her lips together for a moment to regain her composure. "Since

I learned the truth about us, I've dreamed about you several times. You were the one we clung to when we were scared."

Sadie nodded. "I've had dreams like that, too." Her voice wavered. "You would hold me and whisper to me. I didn't know it was you until I heard your voice just now. I was so stunned I couldn't move for a second there." She broke the chain for a moment and swiped her eyes. "I can't believe I have two beautiful sisters!"

The hugging resumed. The tears had never stopped. Olivia glanced at Victoria, who was dabbing at her eyes, as well. When Victoria's gaze bumped into hers, Olivia mouthed the words *thank you*. Victoria smiled and gave her a nod.

"We only have a few minutes," Victoria said eventually, "before Clare is supposed to arrive. We are as prepared for the unexpected as we can be and that will have to do. Are there any questions?"

Olivia looked to her sisters. "Have any of you remembered anything about the terrible things that happened here?"

"I remember the crying and screaming," Sadie said with a visible shiver. "Not very much else."

Laney nodded. "Me, too. I remember the screaming and being afraid. And the darkness of our hiding place."

"The closet," Olivia confirmed with a shiver of her own. "We always hid in our bedroom closet." She summoned her courage. Victoria's sudden intake of breath startled her but Olivia ignored the distraction. She had to get this said before she lost her nerve. "There was another blonde woman here near the end. I think it was Clare's sister, Janet. In one of my nightmares, I find her in bed with Rafe. So I think there was more going on here than the police realized." She held her breath, hoping either Laney or Sadie could confirm what she believed.

"There was a great deal more going on than anyone knew."

Olivia whirled to face the voice. Clare Barker stood in the

doorway leading from the entry hall to the parlor. She wore a pink dress, apparently her signature color. Her hair was mostly gray and much shorter than in the photos from the album Russ had given Olivia. She looked old and weary and… defeated. Emotions Olivia couldn't begin to label crowded in on her.

This was her mother.

"Have you come alone, Clare, as you promised?" Victoria asked.

Laney and Sadie moved up to stand beside Olivia. The compulsion to usher them behind her was instinctive. But they were grown women now. Olivia squared her shoulders. They stood together, equally strong and brave.

Victoria stood a few feet away, positioned between Clare and them. She waited for an answer to her question. Her posture as well as her expression unyielding.

"I'm alone. He dropped me off." Tears streamed down Clare's cheeks. "But that doesn't mean we're safe. He has something planned." She shook her head. "I don't know what but I know for sure we're all supposed to die."

Sadie gasped and reached for Olivia's hand. Olivia felt for Laney's. "What can we do?" Olivia asked.

"He forced me to make the call to you," Clare said to Victoria. "He insisted that we meet here, so I fear it has something to do with the house."

Victoria touched her ear. "Evacuate now," she ordered.

No wonder her breath had caught a minute ago. She was wearing some sort of communication device. She must have gotten the warning that Clare was coming inside. Olivia struggled to pay attention to Victoria's words and actions but she couldn't stop staring at her mother.

To Olivia and the others, Victoria said, "We're moving out of here now."

Clare's expression morphed to one of terror. "I don't know what he'll do if we try to leave the house."

Suddenly the room was filled with four more bodies. All men, none Olivia recognized. Russ had told her backup was hidden in the house.

"The woods behind the house are clear," one of the men said. "We can go out the back." He looked at each one of them in turn. "Stay low. If you hear gunfire, hit the ground."

"Could there be a bomb?" Olivia asked, suddenly remembering her car exploding in the parking lot of that restaurant. Terror ignited in her veins.

"We brought the dogs through," another of the men said. "They detected no explosives in the house."

The first man who'd spoken touched his ear. "Copy that." He looked to Victoria. "Weeden has been contained. We can evacuate the house without worry now."

Clare was shaking her head. "Something's wrong. He wouldn't go down that easily unless he had a backup plan." She gave her head another resolute shake. "He must have someone helping him. He swore we'd never leave here alive."

Dear God. Olivia held on to her sisters' hands. What did they do now?

RUSS EXHALED A BIG BURST of relief when Weeden was restrained and in the back of the police cruiser. He, Joel Hayden and Lyle McCaleb had staked out the road west of the Barker house, while three of Whitt's men had watched the east end that led back to town. They had given Russ a heads-up when Weeden and Clare passed en route to the old Barker place. According to the scout hidden in the woods closest to the highway, Weeden had let Clare out and driven on. Straight into their trap.

Russ had an uneasy feeling that taking him down had been too easy. His gut was in all kinds of knots.

"We've got remote detonators in the car!" Hayden shouted from the sedan Weeden had arrived in. "Five in all!"

Fear burst in Russ's chest. He charged forward, yanked the rear door of the cruiser open and dragged Weeden out. He shoved him against the car and jammed the barrel of his weapon into the soft underside of the bastard's chin. "Where are the bombs?" Behind him, Russ could hear McCaleb informing Simon and Victoria back at the house.

Weeden laughed. His bloody T-shirt and wild, bulging eyes gave him the look of something out of a horror flick. "You're too late."

"There were no bombs found in the house," Russ argued, fury roaring in his brain. He jammed the muzzle harder into the man's throat. "Where are they?"

"Doesn't matter," Weeden sneered. "They're going off and you can't stop them."

"We have the remote detonators," Hayden countered sharply, moving in closer. "They're not doing a damned thing without being detonated."

"There are backup detonators on timers," Weeden said with a laugh. "Another minute max and all those devices buried around the house will go boom!" He laughed again. "You can't do a damned thing because you're here with me!"

"Head into the woods," the man Olivia had learned was Simon Ruhl shouted. "The bombs are buried around the house. We need distance and cover."

Heart and legs pumping, Olivia and her sisters ran for the woods. Hot tears stung her cheeks. What if they didn't make it?

They breached the edge of the woods. Victoria and Clare were right behind them.

"Oh, God."

Olivia stopped and turned around. Victoria was rushing

back out into the open. Olivia's heart seemed to stall. Clare wasn't behind them. She'd fallen to the ground halfway between the house and the woods.

"Victoria! Stop!" Simon rushed past Olivia.

Olivia started after them. To help. She had to help. The men in the woods, cops and Colby investigators, were shouting for her and her sisters to come on. To hurry!

For a moment Olivia was frozen watching Victoria risk her life to save the woman who had been charged with multiple murders more than two decades ago. Another man, this one older and hobbling badly, burst from the tree line on the right. Two others rushed after him.

"We should…" Sadie's voice trailed off.

Her sister's voice snapped Olivia out of the trance. She grabbed her sisters by the hands. "We have to go deeper into the woods."

As they rushed forward, men with guns crowded around them, ushering them into the thickening protection of the trees.

The first blast shook the ground.

"Get down!" one of the men shouted.

They all went flat on the ground, between bushes and saplings, amid the leaves.

Another blast and another… They just kept coming.

Olivia prayed Clare, Victoria and the others were unharmed. *Please don't let anyone die today.*

Finally the violent explosions stopped.

Olivia dared to move up onto her knees. Her ears rung with the silence. Was anyone hurt? Sadie and Laney scrambled over to where she kneeled.

"Are you okay?" Laney asked.

Olivia nodded. "You?" She looked from Laney to Sadie and back. Both nodded.

The officers and investigators who had been in the woods

with them started to move toward the clearing where the house was…if it was still there. One of them stopped long enough to say, "You ladies stay put until we assess the situation."

Olivia got to her feet, her legs rubbery. She dusted off her skirt and wished she had her cell phone so she could make sure Russ was okay. If the bombs were here and Weeden was contained, surely Russ was safe. She tried to see beyond the trees. Clare had fallen and Victoria had rushed to help her. The man named Simon and another man who'd been limping had gone back out there. She hoped they were all okay.

"What's this?"

Sadie was kneeling near one of the stones Olivia and Russ had uncovered. Olivia knelt beside her and touched the angel inscribed there. "The families or someone marked all the sites where remains were found."

Laney joined them. "Oh, my God. I knew that from one of the old newspaper clippings I read but it didn't seem real."

"It was real all right." She gathered her courage once more. "And it's time we knew the whole truth."

With her sisters following her, Olivia walked out of those woods. Her heart skipped a couple of beats when she saw that Clare and Victoria, as well as the others, were safe.

But the house…it had collapsed in on itself. It lay there, broken and splintered, and incapable of harboring any more secrets.

8:15 p.m.

No ONE HAD BEEN INJURED in the blasts. Clare had fallen because she had been weak from the beating Tony Weeden had given her. He'd avoided hitting her in the face. Instead, he'd pummeled her body and banged the back of her head against the floor.

Olivia felt sorry for her. Though she didn't know all the facts, the poor woman had suffered a great deal at the hands of her sister, her husband and then her son.

Laney and Sadie paced the hospital waiting room. Olivia had done that for a while but she was exhausted and her feet were killing her. She considered her high heels and then the boots that her sisters wore. Maybe there was something to be said for Western wear. If invited, she might just spend a few days in the country with one or both and try the cowgirl lifestyle.

She smiled. With her sisters. They were finally together.

Victoria and her husband, Lucas, the man with the cast on his leg, waited with them. Simon Ruhl, Russ and the other members of the Colby team were still at the Granger Police Department where Weeden was confessing his sins. Simon kept Victoria apprised of the developments.

Olivia wished she had been able to stay with Russ, but she'd needed to be here…to hear what Clare would tell them. And to support her sisters. Whatever happened after this, Olivia intended to explore these feelings she had for Russ. Warmth flowed through her, chasing away the awful chills those moments in the woods had generated.

They were all safe. The worst was over.

She hoped.

Tony Weeden had admitted to working with Rafe. Tony had finagled the job at the prison just so he could be close to Rafe. He and Rafe had something in common—they both hated Clare and worshipped Janet on some twisted level. When Rafe learned that Clare's conviction would be overturned, he used Tony's hatred to devise a plan to make her pay the ultimate price.

Rafe had given Tony all sorts of ideas on things to do in order to make Clare look guilty. Like the fire at the apartment complex in Copperas Cove where she'd gone straight from prison. The burning down of Sadie's home and the ugly message that had been left on her door. He'd scared Clare into thinking that the Colby Agency was trying to prove she belonged back in prison and was attempting to keep her daughters from her. He had convinced her that he was the only person who could save her and that Rafe had orchestrated the fire at Sadie's and the one at the complex. He'd convinced Clare that he had saved her.

Weeden had wanted to paint her as totally insane and as a murderer. When first interrogated, he'd insisted that it was all Clare's idea but he'd made one glaring mistake. The ex-con he'd hired to do all the explosives work and the fires, including the one at Keisha Landers's home, wasn't about to leave Granger without payment for the final job so he'd waited at the Boxcar Motel for Weeden to settle with him. In a small community like Granger, every stranger was noticed. With the police on high alert for today's meeting between Clare and her daughters, the stranger at the motel had gotten noticed. All sorts of evidence had been found in his car. He'd given up Weeden before the first question was thrown at him. He'd reminded the cops how he was careful that no one got hurt in any of the fires or the explosions. Of course, the lack of casualties at his final foray at the old Barker house was sheer luck.

Having been employed by the prison system, Weeden had known all sorts of unsavory characters. Those still inside and some out on parole.

Murdering Janet, however, hadn't been a part of Rafe's plan. Weeden killing her had been the result of an emotional scene between two twisted individuals gone completely out of control. She'd feared he might attempt revenge as soon as she learned he was playing the part of go-between for her and Rafe. Truth was, according to Tony, she was jealous of his new standing with Rafe. That was the reason she'd given the photo albums to her neighbor. The locations of Rafe's daughters had given her a certain power that she hadn't wanted to relinquish to Weeden. She'd had a sizable savings stashed in her home and had planned to disappear if things went south where she and Weeden were concerned. And she'd worried that Clare might decide to seek revenge. Janet's one mistake was that she'd trusted Rafe completely until the bitter end. She'd told him about her little nest egg. Weeden had killed her and taken the money. It had provided the funds for his explosives and arson expert as well as the car he'd purchased after the shootout last weekend.

Weeden and Rafe had their revenge against Clare all planned out. Both had wanted her to know she was the reason her daughters had died this day. They were supposed to have died twenty-two years ago as punishment for her tipping off the police. Rafe had discovered that Clare had told the minister of her church everything about what she suspected he and Janet were up to. The minister had made the anonymous tip and he had kept Clare's secret all these years. As Clare's minister he could not divulge the secrets she had shared with him in that capacity.

When Rafe learned what she had done, he tied her up in a closet and had Janet take their daughters away from the house. Janet was supposed to kill the girls and dispose of their bodies. She'd had no qualms about doing the job but she had known the girls would be worth something. So she'd used a lawyer to sell them in private adoptions. She hadn't told Rafe until she learned Clare was going to be released. That was when a new plan had been set in motion. Destroy them all in one fell swoop. He'd hoped to capitalize on the Colby Agency's reputation for compassion and integrity. And that their need to seek out and protect the girls would lead Weeden right to all three.

Janet's greed had put her on Rafe's bad side. The way she had abused Weeden had turned his fear of her as a child to sheer hatred as an adult. He had told the police that she was actually the one to chop off his arm when the Weedens informed her that he'd tried to run away. Janet had reveled in telling him that he was lucky she hadn't chopped him to bits the way she had hers and Clare's parents. He'd vowed to himself that she would one day pay, as would Clare for leaving him with her rotten sister.

But Rafe and Weeden had failed in their ultimate goal.

The double doors marked Authorized Personnel Only swung open and Olivia broke from her disturbing thoughts. Dr. Raby, the E.R. physician who'd been on call, breezed into the lobby for the first time in more than an hour.

Olivia stood as he approached. Her sisters came to her side. The feelings that flooded her at having them with her were nearly overpowering. "How is she?" Her voice trembled but there was no help for that. She was still shaky considering what could have happened at that damned farmhouse and all the wondrous emotions she had been experiencing since.

"She has three fractured ribs and a concussion, but Clare is going to be fine."

Despite scarcely knowing the woman and having thought she was a heinous murderer, Olivia breathed a sigh of relief.

"Can we see her?" Sadie asked.

"Detective Whitt is questioning her," the doctor explained. "He can answer that for you when he's done. There is no medical reason to restrict visitors but I don't know where the police stand on the matter."

"Thank you, Dr. Raby." Olivia produced a smile for him and tried valiantly to stop the trembling in her body.

Victoria and Lucas joined their huddle. "Simon just confirmed that Tony Weeden has been charged with multiple counts of attempted murder as well as murder in the first degree for the death of Terrence Kingston."

Kingston was Laney's little boy's father. Weeden had killed

him and taken the boy. It was a miracle the little boy had been returned to his mother unharmed. Probably only because of Clare's intervention. There Olivia went, giving Clare the benefit of the doubt. Olivia gave herself a mental shake. There were still a lot of unanswered questions from twenty-two years ago. Clare's guilt or innocence, in Olivia's eyes, was still in question.

"That's a relief," Laney said. "No matter that Buddy's father was a jerk, he didn't deserve to be murdered. And his killer definitely shouldn't get away with it."

Olivia hugged Laney. As brave as Laney wanted to appear, Olivia could see that she suffered on the inside with the loss of a man for whom she had obviously once cared.

"Victoria and I are going to the cafeteria for coffee," Lucas said. "Would you ladies care for anything?"

All three declined.

When they were alone, Olivia fixed another, brighter, smile into place. "So, what have you two been up to the last twenty years or so?"

They all laughed and the tension shrank a little. Laney and Sadie filled her in and Olivia had just gotten started when Detective Whitt appeared.

"Clare would like to see the three of you," he announced.

"Is that okay with you?" Olivia held her breath, hoped he wouldn't deny them at least a few minutes.

"It's time the four of you had some time together." Like the rest of them he looked tired and rumpled and relieved. "I've spent the past two decades plus believing that Clare Barker was as guilty as her husband. But it appears I may have been wrong."

Olivia and her sisters waited in stunned silence for him to continue.

"I'll let her tell you her story. I have to hand it to the higher courts, they definitely got it right this time. We made a mistake by coloring her with the same brush we used on Rafe. She has paid a heavy price for that mistake."

"Does that mean she won't face any charges for her complicity in Weeden's actions?" Olivia understood that there were extenuating circumstances. Still, she had been aware that Tony had done certain things that were unquestionably criminal.

"I think I can convince the D.A. to let her off with a year in a recovery center. After what she's been through I suspect some time in real counseling and with structured daily activities will help her to transition back into society. There's a very good place just outside Houston. She'll have her own small apartment and she can have visitors but she'll get the help she needs to come to terms with the bad hand she was dealt in the past. For now, the hospital is keeping her overnight for observation considering what she's been through mentally and physically."

"That's an excellent idea." Olivia was relieved that he had come to that conclusion. "Thank you, Detective." She had been so wrong about him. Justice was often difficult to bring about under such puzzling and emotional circumstances as all involved faced twenty-two years ago.

He gestured to the doors. "Let the desk nurse know and she'll buzz you ladies back."

As they passed through those foreboding doors, the Barker sisters held hands. They would face this together as they would likely face much more together, both good and bad, in the future. It was a genuine relief to know that Clare had not been a part of those tragic murders. But they had a long ways to go before Clare would feel like family.

Clare's eyes were closed when they entered the room. She looked as pale as the white sheet covering her. Soon she would be transferred to a room for her overnight stay. Olivia suspected the observation was more for monitoring her mental state than the concussion.

When the door closed behind them Clare's eyes opened. Her lips trembled into a smile. "I was afraid you wouldn't want to see me."

Sadie and Laney looked to Olivia to speak first. "We wouldn't leave without seeing you first."

"Thank you." She fiddled with the sheet. "I don't deserve your compassion."

Sadie moved to her bedside first. She reached out and took her hand. "Are you comfortable? Did they give you something for the pain?"

More of those hot tears slid down Olivia's cheeks. She and Laney exchanged a look and then they both went to Clare's side. It would take time and there would be many bumps on the road, but they would find their place together.

Clare told them the story of how she'd had no idea her husband was a murderer. He'd always seemed so kind and caring. Until Janet showed up in their lives. She and Rafe would drink and behave badly. Clare looked away when she told them that part. It was still hard for her to believe that he'd been doing those awful things for most of their marriage. She felt like a fool for not recognizing that side of him. Olivia and her sisters didn't ask any questions.

"I don't know," Clare said, "if it was the alcohol or her, but something made those evil urges of his escalate." She looked from one of her daughters to the next. "That's when I knew something was wrong. He and Janet would come home in the middle of the night. They'd have blood all over them. I didn't know what to think. The way they were acting I was afraid to ask. The next morning he would tell me that he'd rescued some animal or done some sort of emergency surgery to explain his bloody clothes. Lies." She shook her head. "All of it. They were out hunting little girls to slaughter. When I tried to question Janet, she warned what she would do if I made trouble for her." Clare's gaze settled on each of her daughter's in turn. "She threatened to hurt you girls. She watched everything I did. I was trapped for those four long months after she showed up. I couldn't run without leaving the three of you behind and that was out of the question. Finally, I took that chance by telling my minister what I suspected and all hell broke loose. Janet had been following me. She didn't know what I told him but she knew I told him something. She and Rafe went into a frenzy." She closed her eyes ad shook her head. "I was terrified for you girls."

Olivia cleared the lump of emotion from her throat. "I saw you cleaning up blood from the floor once." Remembering that scene in a dream had made Olivia believe that Clare had been involved in the murders or that, at the very least, she had known about them.

"Janet got injured somehow on one of their outings. I found her on your bedroom floor the next morning. By the time I got her patched up and in bed in the guest room and returned to clean up the mess, the three of you had gotten up, seen the blood and hidden in the closet. You were scared to death. I tried to assure you everything was okay. But it wasn't. It was never okay. I was just too blind to see it until the end."

"Why did Janet try to hurt you so?" Laney wanted to know.

Clare reached for Laney's hand. "She hated me. When I was born she thought our parents loved me more so she tried to drown me. After several attempts to kill me, my parents sent her away to live with another family."

Clare blinked at the emotion shining in her eyes. "A part of me always suspected she was the one who murdered them, but I couldn't be sure and she never said. When she helped me with Tony, I thought maybe I'd been wrong about her all that time. But I know now that she only did that to hurt me more. She did terrible things to him and the people she sold him to were even worse. He's not entirely to blame for how he turned out. I'm responsible in large part."

She sighed mightily. "When she learned I was happily married with three beautiful daughters she wanted to ruin that, too. Discovering that she and Rafe shared evil urges was just icing on her poison cake. God only knows what they did with the bodies of those girls they murdered. Rafe won't ever tell. I guess we'll never know."

They talked for a long time. Many tears were shed, but in the end it was a new beginning for them all.

And the secrets of the past were finally revealed for Olivia and her sisters. Now they could try to move on with their lives.

It wouldn't be easy. There was a lot of healing ahead of them. But Olivia knew exactly where she wanted to start.

Chapter Nineteen

10:30 p.m.

Russ couldn't sit still. He had paced the hospital lobby for the past hour. McCaleb and Hayden had done the same. They'd driven back to the hospital as soon as Weeden's interrogation and booking was complete. When they arrived, Victoria explained that Olivia and her sisters were talking to Clare. Russ had been losing his mind ever since.

The sinking feeling that had about stolen his legs from under him when he heard the first explosion would haunt him for the rest of his life. They had intercepted Weeden about a half of a mile from the old Barker place and even at that distance they had heard the explosions as if they were right on top of them. Not knowing if anyone was injured had ripped his heart from his chest.

As soon as he heard that Olivia and everyone were safe he'd been able to breathe again. It had taken every ounce of restraint he possessed not to beat the hell out of Weeden then and there.

Now that bastard would end up on death row like his pal Rafe. Only Rafe wouldn't last long enough for a reunion. Victoria had told them that Olivia had called her boss and told him to withdraw the petition, considering Weeden's confession of Rafe's part in this latest travesty. Detective Whitt had spoken to him, as well. The three had ultimately had a conference call with the D.A. and the Governor. Rafe's execution would be carried out as scheduled.

Now Olivia and her sisters could move forward toward getting to know each other without all those questions hanging over their heads. Russ hoped Olivia felt the way he did about his being a part of her future. It was hard to believe they'd only been together a few days. But he'd been watching her a lot longer than that and the truth was he'd fallen for her just a little before they'd even exchanged a word.

As if his thoughts had summoned her she walked right up to him and smiled. His heart took a leap.

"Hey," she said.

"Hey," he said back, his insides shaking with anticipation.

Laney and Hayden were hugging, as were Sadie and Mc-Caleb. Both couples were engaged. Made Russ a little jealous, even though he was happy for them. If he had his way, he would fix that in the very near future.

Olivia looped her arm in his and pulled him close. "We're the only ones out here who aren't getting married," she whispered. "I'm now scheduled to be a bridesmaid twice in as many months. I've never been a bridesmaid before." She smiled again but her eyes told the tale. She was wondering where they went from here, as well.

Russ leaned closer to her, loving the electricity that instantly sparked. "You'll love it. And since I'm a groomsman, we'll have to make sure we get to walk together." Practice, he wanted to add.

She lifted a skeptical eyebrow. "I don't know about the loving-it part. Since both their mothers are gone, I think they're expecting me to be in charge of the wedding plans. I've seen movies about how crazy that can get." She shrugged. "I suppose as long as it doesn't include taffeta I might survive."

They shared a nervous laugh. God, he just wanted to pull

her into his arms and kiss her right there. Instead, he worried about whether or not she had ever considered marriage in her future. "You should be proud to have that honor."

Her cheeks flushed as she chewed on her lower lip. "I guess I am. I just never expected to be in a wedding period."

"Not even your own?" he ventured, his nerves vibrating with uncertainty. He wanted to show this woman just how good the right relationship could be. He wanted that chance more than he'd ever wanted anything.

"Especially not my own." She laughed, the sound as nervous as he felt. "Remember I'm the woman who doesn't know how to have a relationship."

He put his hand over hers and squeezed. It was time to man up and pop the first preliminary question. "I thought we were going to change that."

She smiled up at him, her eyes hopeful. "I was afraid you might have changed your mind now that your assignment is over and things are back to normal. Not that anything about my life will ever be completely normal. I'm fully aware that people do and say things in the heat of the moment that they regret later. If you want to rescind the offer now I understand. I'm not exactly a safe bet in the relationship department."

He kissed her. It was the only way to show her in no uncertain terms that he had no intention of retracting anything. Her arms went around his neck and his went around her waist. It was the perfect fit. He had no intention of letting this lady go. She hadn't been the easiest filly to round up but she was his now.

Applause echoed around them. They drew apart and Olivia's cheeks turned a deeper red as her sisters and their fiancés continued to clap loudly and cheered them on.

"Looks like it's official," Russ warned her.

"What's that?" she asked, that uncertainty still shining in her eyes.

"Your sisters approve. We can't let them down."

"So where do we go from here?"

"My place," he said with a wink.

"And after that?" She toyed with a button on his shirt, still obviously a little skittish when it came to putting her hopes in the future of a relationship.

"We'll work that out as we go. There's no hurry. As long as we're committed, the rest will fall into place."

She turned those big brown eyes up to him and the uncertainty was gone. "I'm definitely committed."

He grinned. "That makes two of us."

She made a face that warned she was worried about how he would take what she had to say next. "I was thinking about going back to law school and finishing that final year."

"If that's what you want, I'll back you one-hundred percent. Never doubt that, Liv. I'm with you, whatever we do and wherever we go."

Her relief was palpable. "My reason for walking away was a cop-out." She shrugged. "Another one of those commitment issues. But I'm not afraid anymore. Not with you backing me up."

"That's my girl."

Olivia rose up on tiptoe and kissed him. More of that zany applause broke out behind them.

Russ intended to take the lady home with him and spend the rest of his days showing her how good life and the right relationship could be.

VICTORIA WAS IMMENSELY thankful they were almost home. She refused to let Lucas drive with that cast. He'd finally stopped arguing and settled in for the three-hour trip.

They'd chatted about how thankful they were that the facts in the Princess Killer case had been brought to light once and for all. They'd even discussed the possibility of Russ and Olivia joining the ranks of the engaged. It seemed that the Colby Agency had facilitated the love lives of three happy couples.

She sighed. She loved it when things turned out exactly right.

"Did I tell you that Casey called?" Lucas said.

He knew perfectly well he had not. "When did he call?" Thomas Casey was one of Lucas's oldest and dearest friends, as well as his former boss from their CIA days.

"Oh, yesterday or the day before."

Lucas was still annoyed that she was pushing the issue of total retirement. The truth was, she loved being a part of the cases that came into the Colby Agency. The trouble was, Lucas too often ended up in danger. She would not allow him to continue to risk his life for anything.

"What did Thomas have to say?" Thomas Casey's niece, Casey Manning, had helped Levi Stark, one of Victoria's investigators from the Chicago office, with an investigation last fall into the troubles with Lucas's son, Slade Keaton. Casey and Levi had fallen in love and had been together since.

"His niece Casey is getting married next spring."

Why hadn't Victoria heard about this? Levi hadn't said a word. Of course, she had been down here in Texas and rather busy. "That's wonderful."

"As soon as the arrangements are final he'll let us know. We're at the top of the guest list, of course."

"Of course."

"He also asked me to consider doing some advising with his team later this year. I told him I would think about it."

Victoria held her tongue until the wave of frustration had eased to a tolerable level. "You worked in an advisory capacity in D.C. for many years, Lucas. I thought those days were over." She wanted him at her side. Safe.

"I can't deny that I miss the fulfillment of helping with a top-secret mission that involves national security."

And there it was. The bare truth. He did not want to retire.

"So you don't want to retire, after all?" She hated that disappointment weighted her words but there was no help for it.

"Victoria, this whole business about retirement has been about you being afraid I would be hurt."

That was true. She couldn't deny it.

"And we both know that could happen getting out of the shower in the morning."

"Let's not compare work with the CIA to getting out of the shower, Lucas."

"It could happen rushing back to help someone who had fallen, despite knowing that bombs were buried in that area."

He had her. "Yes, yes, I rushed back to help Clare with no thought to the danger to myself." It was true and she would do it again. "I know this about both of us, Lucas. And it terrifies me. I just want us to be a normal couple with a normal life."

He laughed long and loud.

"I see absolutely nothing amusing. I'm completely serious."

"Pull over, my dear."

"What? Now?"

"Yes."

Since they had left the interstate behind, his request wasn't a problem. She turned into the parking lot of the next convenience store. She put the car in Park and turned to him.

He leaned over the console and took her face in his hands. "Victoria, we are not normal people. We will never be normal people. We have a calling, and to deny that calling is to live in fear or avoidance and that would only make us unhappy and resentful. It's far better that we embrace who we are and what we do."

"But what about traveling and spending time just the two of us?"

"That we will do, I promise you. What we need in our lives now is balance. We can achieve that without giving up our calling. When we're needed on a special case, like this one, we'll be there. The rest of our time will be ours to do with as we please. Does that sound like an acceptable compromise?"

Victoria smiled. "It's more than acceptable. It's brilliant."

Lucas kissed her and Victoria understood that this was exactly what they were supposed to do for the rest of their lives.

* * * * *

Dear Reader,

I really hope you enjoyed the fiftieth story in the Colby Agency series! Last year, as I neared that milestone, I began to think about what I might be able to give all of you as a special thank-you for being such loyal friends of the Colby Agency. After much discussion and planning, Harlequin, my terrific editor and I came upon the perfect idea—a companion guide to all fifty Colby books!

I know many of you have followed the series from book one, but some have joined our journey along the way. Over the years I have gotten many questions about which characters were in what books. So I am pleased to say that the official Colby Companion Guide is our gift to you in this fiftieth installment of the Colby Agency series.

Enjoy!

Debra Webb

The Colby Agency

A Companion Guide

Safe by His Side—#1

Harlequin Intrigue

The Colby Agency began with this first book. Victoria Colby, head of the agency, and Lucas Camp were introduced along with Nick Foster, the hero of book two. The story revolved around the enigmatic Jack Raine and the determined Katherine Robertson.

No one could find special agent Jack Raine if he didn't want to be found. So who was the beautiful amnesiac on his doorstep, and how had she gotten to his hideaway? When a killer soon followed, Jack suspected a trap—so he took the lady and ran....

Katherine "Kate" couldn't remember her own name, but she wanted the strong and silent Jack Raine the moment she saw him. Even as a slow heat burned between them, Kate knew she risked falling for this stranger who'd saved her life—a man her flashes of memory suggested she might have been sent to capture....

As the story concluded, Kate and Jack got married during a private ceremony at a tiny wedding chapel in the Smoky Mountains before moving to Jack's house in Virginia. Both left their jobs (hers at the Colby Agency and his at the CIA's new Special Ops division). Both Victoria and Lucas attended the wedding and laughingly blamed the other for losing one of their best agents!

Raine is still advising various government entities from

time to time, but mostly he spends time with his two children. Katherine is absolutely satisfied with being a stay-at-home mom and a loving wife to Raine. Her father recently moved into a small cabin next door and loves being a full-time grandfather.

The Bodyguard's Baby—#2

Harlequin Intrigue

Book two introduced Nick Foster and Laura Proctor, along with her sweet son, Robby (who was named for my eldest nephew!). Ian Michaels, who still works with Victoria forty-eight books later, also made his unforgettable entrance in this story.

Nick had been fully prepared to give his life to protect Laura's. And that's what it almost cost the handsome body-guard. Laura Proctor was more than a job to Nick—and they had unfinished business. For two years Laura was suspected dead. Nick hadn't believed it. But he also *couldn't* believe she'd had a baby in that time…with anyone else but him.

Laura would trust Nick with her life, but not with her se-cret. And she wouldn't go back to Jackson, Mississippi, with him and leave her child in the hands of a kidnapper. Somehow she had to convince Nick that her baby was missing, but that the child *wasn't* his. Because the closer he got to the truth, the more danger would come to them all.

As the story concluded, Nick and Laura decided to get married. Neither could picture life without the other, and together they would raise little Robby! Nick decided to take an extended leave of absence from the Colby Agency to be with his wife and son. Eventually he left the agency in order to pursue a quiet life with Laura and their son. Since leaving the Colby Agency, Nick has pursued a career in developing a state-of-the-art security system for residential use. He and Laura welcome a second child into their family.

Protective Custody—#3

Harlequin Intrigue

Ian Michaels was Victoria's second-in-command and one of the best investigators at the Colby Agency—also one of the most gorgeous. Nicole Reed knew all too well just how good Ian could be. Together they had worked to protect a federal witness. In close quarters, desire erupted and ultimately played a role in the death of their client. Or so Ian thought. But it was Nicole who had been sent to see that Ian—the best protector money could buy—failed and that the witness was secreted into hiding. Losing her heart to Ian wasn't part of the assignment.

Now in order to stay alive, Nicole needed the help of the man she once betrayed. Only, this time, would that all-consuming passion cause Nicole's and Ian's demise?

Ian and Nicole move in together in Chicago (Nicole's apartment had gone up in flames) and are pregnant! They are 90 percent positive it's a girl. They both remain at the Colby Agency as two of Victoria's top investigators. They eventually have a second daughter.

Solitary Soldier—#4

Harlequin Intrigue

She'd heard his heart was as hard as his honed body and as cold as the steel of his gun. But the man called Sloan was Rachel Larson's last hope. She had nowhere else to hide from her son's father—a cold-blooded assassin, and Sloan's deadliest enemy. So she faced this lone wolf in his lair and pleaded for his help.

Ex-Colby investigator Sloan lived only to take down the man who'd killed all he loved, including his own son. Now a desperate, desirable woman offered him that chance on a silver platter. Vengeance was his—if he could keep Rachel and her son from invading the fortress around his heart....

By story's end Sloan came to New Orleans and proposed to Rachel. She accepted his offer of marriage. Sloan promised to raise and love Rachel's son just as he did his own! These days Sloan is retired. He and Rachel live in Mexico and homeschool their two children. They spend much of their time working to make life better for those less fortunate. After an unfortunate miscarriage they have a third child.

Personal Protector—#5

Harlequin Intrigue

Atlanta's most beloved news reporter wanted her new cameraman fired. Why? Because she couldn't even glance at the sexy Latino without wanting to touch him to see if he felt as hot as he looked. He was a distraction she couldn't afford... not when her first priority was staying alive.

But what Piper didn't know just might save her life. Because Ric Martinez was more than just a cocky cameraman with a knack for protecting Piper and making her melt with desire. He was an undercover Colby investigator on the biggest bodyguard assignment of his career: her!

Ric and Piper get married and are going to live in Chicago! Ric will return to the Colby Agency after he and Piper take some time together. Ric is still a mover and a shaker at the Colby Agency. He and Piper have tied the knot but don't plan to have children for a while. Piper has become a household name in Chicago as the princess of investigative journalism.

Physical Evidence—#6

Harlequin Intrigue

Nobody came to Mitch Hayden's county and caused trouble—least of all a fancy-pants lady P.I. from the big city. And Sheriff Hayden was nothing if not a man of his word. But Alexandra "Alex" Preston made a liar out of him with her blank memory and maddening allure. She'd come to town to investigate a missing-person case, and ended up a prime suspect in the murder of one of Mitch's deputies. Though all evidence pointed to Alex, Mitch believed otherwise. So was his lawman mettle on the fritz...or was his physical knowledge of Alex suspect?

Victoria hates to lose a good Colby investigator like Alex, but the kind of love Alex and Mitch have found doesn't come along every day. Instead of trying to make a long-distance relationship work, Mitch and Alex decide to settle in Tennessee. The two marry and Mitch remains sheriff while Alex does a little selective private-investigation work locally in Raleigh County. The happily married couple have a beautiful daughter!

The Marriage Prescription—#7

Harlequin American Romance

Operation: Seduction. As a love-struck teen, Beth McCormick had offered her innocence to Zach Ashton...only to have him turn her away. Now, years later, he returned to their one-horse hometown, a successful legal crusader legendary with the ladies and less attainable than ever....

But then, Beth wanted only one night.

One night to make Zach see her as a seductive woman and not the sweet lady doctor next door. One night to exorcise the man of her dreams from her system forever. But Beth underestimated her heart...and her childhood hero. Because Zach was a master at turnaround—and a man with an agenda of his own....

Beth and Zach get married in a beautiful October wedding and their son's name is Charles Zacharius Ashton III. He is christened in a Catholic cathedral with the most important people in his parents' lives there, including many friends from the Colby Agency. They end up having two beautiful children and find the perfect house in the suburbs near Chicago. Beth is practicing medicine at Chicago General and Zach is a stay-at-home dad, advising on cases at the Colby Agency once in a great while—like when Victoria's son was in trouble.

Zach and Beth both move their moms to Chicago to be near their grandchildren. The two women still bicker over who will do what with which child first.

Contract Bride—#8

Harlequin Intrigue

Bride-to-be…murdered?

Jennifer Ballard never anticipated her wedding day to be an intricate setup. Her fiancé plotted to kill her, then take over her family pharmaceuticals business—and Jennifer's first instinct was to turn to the prestigious Colby Agency for help. Suddenly she found herself under the protection of Ethan Delaney, the larger-than-life investigator assigned to her case. But in the midst of their clandestine mission to uncover the conspiracy that threatened to destroy her life, Jennifer was unwittingly drawn to her tough-as-nails bodyguard. With only each other to trust, they had to overcome danger—and desire—to unravel the dangerous plot.

Ethan and Jenn marry and have their first child. Ethan stays on with the Colby Agency, but is extra cautious now because Jenn wants him around for a long, long time! Dr. Austin Ballard begins dating the Colby Agency's Mildred Parker, Victoria's personal assistant. Ethan and Jenn eventually begin working side by side at the Colby Agency. In time they welcome the birth of twin boys and Mildred plays surrogate grandmother.

From an Interoffice Memo from Victoria: Marriages announced: Katherine Robertson and Jack Raine, Nick Foster and Laura Proctor, Ian Michaels and Nicole

Reed, Trevor Sloan and Rachel Larson, Ric Martinez and Piper Ryan, Alex Preston and Mitch Hayden, and Zach Ashton and Elizabeth McCormick! Who will be next? Perhaps Mildred Parker and Austin Ballard!

Undercover Wife—#9

Harlequin Intrigue—The Specialists

Mission Recovery "Special Operations." When all else fails, a Specialist is called in to "recover" a situation.

This team of highly skilled men and women was created to serve the needs of all other U.S. Government agencies whenever the usual channels failed. The elite force is trained in every area of antiterrorism and aggressive infiltration and headed by Thomas Casey and Lucas Camp. All agents have extensive stealth and sniper training and are multilingual. They must meet the most stringent mental and physical requirements of any national or international security force. They are prepared to do *whatever* it takes to accomplish their mission. Failure is not an option.

Specialist John Logan was dedicated to duty—the mission always top priority—and he'd do anything to carry out an assignment. Even if it meant posing as the unthinkable—husband to the newly "recruited" Erin Bailey.

He'd shown up in the middle of the night and offered Erin her freedom *if* she'd pose as his wife to catch an insidious drug lord/arms dealer. Except, giving the compromising position she found herself in as victim of a frame-up, Erin was totally at the mercy of her "guardian" as an untrained, stand-in agent. All she had to do was assume someone else's identity, learn the ins and outs of weaponry *and* share a bed with her dangerously attractive "husband," John Logan. And if she came out of this mess with her life intact, she'd surely lose her heart in the process.

When the case is closed, John and Erin get engaged and become partners in Lucas's elite team.

Her Hidden Truth—#10

Harlequin Intrigue—The Specialists

The mission was always top priority for a Specialist—except this assignment was personal for agent Vince Ferrelli. Though anyone would be hard-pressed to find a tougher operative, Vince had one vulnerability...Katrina Moore.

"Kat" had been fitted with a new memory implant to protect her identity while undercover. But the device malfunctioned and put her in serious jeopardy. Only Vince could extract her from the demented organization—if she remembered the love she'd shared with Vince...and not the truth.

But pretending that they were a passionate couple would be torture for Vince. Because he still loved Kat. And he sure hoped she wouldn't kill him when this case was closed.

Once the mission is recovered, Kat and Vince realize they are still in love and confess it. They marry and have a son.

Guardian of the Night—#11

Harlequin Intrigue—The Specialists

It was just the two of them in the darkness....

Former military intelligence officer Noah Drake exiled himself to a small island off the coast of Georgia after the side effects of an untested drug destroyed his body's tolerance to light. But because of his sacrifice, he brought down a dangerous traitor. Five years later, Noah's adversary was back to settle the score.

The man moved as stealthily as a shadow, but Specialist Maggie "Blue" Callahan had her assignment—to protect Noah at all costs. And no matter how much Noah protested, she would carry it out. Except that was becoming increasingly difficult with the seductive siren call of the night. Would its inexorable rhythm sentence them both to the all-consuming darkness?

Noah and Blue decide that the best assignment for them is one that includes saying "I do!" To make their partnership complete, Noah signs on as a Specialist.

Her Secret Alibi—#12

Harlequin Intrigue

Jolie Randolph worried that she might be losing her mind. That would explain why the typically focused bank executive had discovered inconsistencies in her usually meticulous work, had totally forgotten a business trip and had woken up in a stranger's bed! Jolie was coming undone and was under investigation by the disarmingly handsome Simon Ruhl. But would he book her or bed her?

Undercover Colby investigator Simon Ruhl had his sights set on Jolie for more than one reason. She was suspected in a money-laundering scheme *and* she was clearly being set up. Simon was duty bound to protect Jolie from an unknown threat while surreptitiously proving her innocence—all before he went totally insane with desire for her.

When the case is solved Simon and Jolie get married. They live happily for several years in Chicago and have two gorgeous children. When the Colby Agency decides to branch out with a Texas office, Victoria asks Simon to take the helm of this new division. Simon and family have settled in Houston and the new office is up and running!

Keeping Baby Safe—#13

Harlequin Intrigue

Bounty hunter Olivia "Scout" Jackson was no stranger to danger—but being pregnant changed everything. And wanting, trusting, kissing Pierce Maxwell was risking more than she dared. She couldn't exactly call him a stranger—not when he'd saved her life, not when they'd bared their souls to one another and made love with reckless abandon during what they thought were the last days of their lives. But could she trust the devastating Colby Agency operative to protect her and the precious life she carried when he was duty-bound to her enemy? Or would his loyalties change when he found out he was about to become a father?

Scout and Max get married! The two are loyal investigators at the Colby Agency part-time. They spend the rest of their time with their child and are working on child number two.

Guarding the Heiress—#14

Harlequin American Romance

Doug Cooper's first major assignment with the prestigious Colby Agency: protect the newly discovered D'Martine heiress and turn her into a lady. The tough-as-nails bodyguard had his hands full with Eddi Harper, who was more tomboy than princess and preferred baggy overalls to designer gowns. But during the long days and nights he spent instructing her, the small-town beauty innocently breached the walls he'd erected around his heart, though Doug tried to remain professionally detached, keeping his distance. Doug swore he'd stop at nothing to guard the heiress, but who was going to guard his heart?

Doug and Eddi are happily married with a beautiful baby girl! Doug left the Colby Agency to work with Eddi at the D'Martine jewel business. Eddi's father sold his hardware business and he and Eddi's mother are very involved in the D'Martine ventures, as well, making for one big happy family.

Cries in the Night—#15

Harlequin Intrigue

Haunted by her daughter's cries in the night, Melany Jackson would stop at nothing to track down her precious child. And if that meant joining forces with Colby investigator Ryan Braxton—the man she still desperately loved—then so be it. But what Melany feared even more than her electrifying response to Ryan's potent masculinity was that he'd discover her child belonged to him. Without a second to spare, they frantically unraveled the maze of clues in this confounding case. Their shared desperation unleashed a frenzied passion that threatened to consume them both. But each step they took toward rescuing the child brought Ryan closer to an undeniable truth that could shatter their future....

Melany and Ryan are happily married, living in Chicago. Their daughter, Katlin, is thriving. Ryan is still with the Colby Agency. Melany has started working at the Colby Agency's research department part-time since Katlin started school.

Striking Distance—#16

Harlequin Special Release

CIA recruit Tasha North was assigned to draw out an unknown assassin and neutralize him—to take whatever risks were required to accomplish her assignment. The ruthless killing machine had no conscience, no fear and a black hole for a heart, and he had targeted the dynamic head of the Colby private investigation agency for termination. But Tasha was determined to stop him at all costs.

Tasha soon realized carnal seduction was the only way to reach the suspected killer. Years of rage and fantasies of revenge had destroyed any semblance of human emotion in him. Yet when he took Tasha in his arms, the two connected in the most basic man-woman way. Penetrating his personal fortress was the only hope she had…and she'd have to use her own heart as bait.

Many of Victoria's dreams come true in the culmination of this story. The man Tasha North was assigned to lure out was called Seth. But in truth he is none other than James "Jim" Colby, Jr.! After eighteen years he is back home again. Although it is a long road to recovery for him, Tasha is at his side every step of the way and so is his mother, Victoria. Tasha and Jim have a daughter, Jamie, and a son, Luke. The two remain in Chicago, where Jim now runs the agency while his mother and Lucas spend time at both the Chicago office and the Texas office.

With Errol Leberman, the Colby family's archenemy, and the past dead and buried, Victoria Colby and Lucas Camp are finally married. She is now Victoria Colby-Camp.

Romancing the Tycoon—#17

Harlequin American Romance

More than anything else, Amy Wells wanted to be a Colby agency investigator, not some administrative assistant filing paper for the best in the business. She knew she'd be good at it. Driven, daring and with a heap of self-confidence, she had what it took to bring down the bad guys. Now, if only she could convince her boss…

When Amy was entangled in a case of mistaken identity, she suddenly found herself on her first assignment—figure out what made gorgeous oil tycoon John Robert Calhoun IV tick. Out of loyalty to his father—and with the country's oil at stake—he was about to agree to an arranged marriage to seal the merger of a lifetime. But what skeletons was he hiding? And what should Amy do about her attraction to the Texas cowboy who had wrangled her heart?

Amy and John have a big Texas wedding. The two commute aboard John's private jet between Dallas and Chicago. Amy loves being a Colby Agency investigator and John is still running his ranch and the family oil business. John's father is campaigning for a grandchild, but for now Amy and John are happy with things just the way they are. However, a recent checkup shook things up when Amy learned she was expecting their first child. Congratulations, Amy and John!

Agent Cowboy—#18

Harlequin Intrigue

In jeopardy and running for her life, Kelly Parker was the lone witness to a ghastly triple murder. Her only chance for survival rested on the impossibly broad shoulders of Trent Tucker. His mission: protect Kelly from a deadly threat while unraveling the clues of a complicated case.

Though the former bounty hunter turned Colby investigator knew he should keep his professional distance from Kelly, his feelings for the young beauty became increasingly personal. But would the combustible passion that raged between them be extinguished by the killer on their trail?

When the case was solved and Kelly was safe, she and Trent took their vows. They live in Texas on the family ranch. Trent helps the Colby Agency whenever they need him for backup in the Lone Star state. The first Tucker child was born on Christmas Day.

Situation: Out of Control—#19

Harlequin Intrigue

The newest addition to the Colby Agency team was assigned the most difficult mission: use all means necessary to eliminate a ruthless mercenary who'd infiltrated the firm, starting with the man's daughter, Jayne Stephens. But Heath Murphy did the unthinkable and got involved with his target—a woman off-limits, a woman he had to protect from her own flesh and blood. As the snow swirled in the remote Colorado mountains, Heath and Jayne became unlikely partners and lovers. But who would be left standing once dawn broke…?

Heath and Jayne married and still live above the Altitude Bar and Grill in Aspen. Heath works side by side with Jayne, giving guided tours to the thousands of tourists who flock to the snow-laden city each winter. Jayne's friends and teammates have accepted Heath as one of their own. Jayne and Heath started a family last year with a precious little girl.

Full Exposure—#20

Harlequin Intrigue

Specialist Cole Danes's investigation revealed the unthinkable—a trusted longtime personal assistant to Victoria Colby had been the source leaking highly sensitive information that could have resulted in the agency's destruction. But it soon became clear that a secondary party was the real culprit. Single mom Angel Parker was being manipulated and controlled by a sinister mercenary driven to destroy the Colby Agency using any means necessary. Her daughter Mia's life was at stake!

Cole was determined to complete his mission, and to accomplish that end he needed Angel. But he didn't expect to *need* Angel.... He had every intention of being as ruthless as his adversaries and using Angel as his pawn, but spending time in seclusion with her wore away his emotional armor. Now he was more concerned with protection than retribution, which could prove fatal for them both.

Cole still works for a highly classified government agency in an advisory capacity, but never strays far from the small home he and Angel share outside Chicago. Cole loves Mia as if she were his own child. He and Angel also now have a son.

Colby Conspiracy—#21

Harlequin Special Release

Victoria Colby-Camp was stunned by the murder of a Chicago police detective who had close ties to her family and her private investigation agency. She decided there was only one man tough and objective enough to clear her name and the agency's reputation. With the keen instincts of a professional, Daniel Marks began digging into Victoria's past, and into that of her long-dead husband…whose last days could be the key to the case.

Daniel reluctantly took on an unofficial partner, Emily Hastings, the daughter of the murdered cop—a woman determined to find her father's killer. Emily found evidence linking her father to Victoria's late husband, as well as discovering the treachery and madness that nearly destroyed Victoria's son, Jim. And as the truth began to emerge, it became clear that a previously unknown and ruthless Colby enemy wanted certain secrets to stay buried….

Once the case was solved, Emily and Daniel took things slowly. Both had their reasons for needing time. But time showed that they were deeply in love. The two married and now live in Chicago with their three rambunctious children.

Investigating 101—#22

Harlequin Intrigue

Todd Thompson had been given the greatest opportunity of his new career—a chance for a permanent position at the prestigious Colby Agency. His assignment: to locate a prominent geneticist's missing and pregnant wife.

Trouble was, working side by side with Serena Blake—the brainy beauty who suspected foul play—provoked certain feelings Todd couldn't ignore. And when a series of mysterious incidents put Serena in jeopardy, Todd vowed he'd stop at nothing to keep her safe.... But now, as the danger escalated around them, the hunt for a sinister criminal threatened to resurrect long-buried secrets that could threaten Todd and Serena's future.

Serena and Todd solve the mystery and decide that there is nothing mysterious about how they feel. The two marry six months later and have a little girl.

Raw Talent—#23

Harlequin Intrigue

When a confidential file was stolen from the prestigious Colby Agency, it was A. J. Braddock's mission to retrieve it. His assignment: locate Gabrielle Jordan, the enigmatic woman who'd vanished with the file. Except he never expected to find her hiding out in Mexico, safeguarding two boys after a failed kidnapping plot at the home of Trevor Sloan. Gabrielle's fierce tenderness toward the youngsters stirred the former military man's own protective instincts. Forced to rely on each other to stay alive, neither could resist the passion that simmered between them—leaving A.J. torn between duty and desire.

Gabrielle comes to terms with her past when the facts are brought to light. She and A.J. are now married but have decided children can wait a while longer.

The Hidden Heir—#24

Harlequin Intrigue

Ashley Orrick would protect her son at all costs. But escaping her all-powerful ex, whose infinite resources seemed almost impossible to elude, was one thing—shaking Victoria Colby-Camp and her exceptional investigators was another. One way or another Ashley had to protect her son from his devious father.

Keith Devers had finally made the leap from analyst to investigator, only to be presented with a conflict of interest. Something didn't add up about Ashley. Was it her long scarlet hair or emerald-green eyes? Or was there something to her story about her ex-husband? Her desperation and maternal ferocity made Keith break all the rules. Fleeing from danger could get them only so far from the one thing they couldn't escape—runaway passions.

Keith retired from the Colby agency after Ashley proposed to him! Another happy ending with this little family.

A Colby Christmas—#25

Harlequin Intrigue

It was number twenty-five with the Colby agency...but would they close the file before Christmas morning came?

Golden boy Brad Gibson never expected that his climb up the corporate ladder would involve dodging bullets. But after he discovered corruption at a leading financial firm, someone wanted his head. Even worse, he feared he was about to lose an exciting opportunity to join the Colby Agency. Now on Christmas Eve he was locked inside a skyscraper equipped with a state-of-the-art security system alongside Colby Agency receptionist Elaine Younger, a doe-eyed beauty not to be underestimated. But with four masked men intent on bringing the agency to its knees, it was going to be a long night of gunfire and dangling mistletoe before Christmas dawned on the most dangerous couple in Chicago.

Brad and Elaine solve the case and save the day—if not the Colby Agency building. Brad and Elaine are married now. They work in the Colby Agency research department and have two lovely kids of their own.

A Soldier's Oath—#26

Harlequin Intrigue–The Equalizers

Willow Harris needed someone who was willing to go beyond the law to get her son back. It was a dangerous mission in a foreign land against ruthless kidnappers who had her son. Hope was all Willow had…until she found the Equalizers.

Spencer Anders might have been new to the Equalizers, but he was a proven professional. Specializing in hostage retrieval, Spencer had earned his stripes overseas. Now with Willow in on the mission, anything could happen—things he couldn't control. The only thing Spencer knew for sure: surrender was not an option.

Willow and her son, Ata, moved to Chicago to be near Spencer. They eventually married and had a sister for Ata. Victoria's assistant, Mildred Parker, and Dr. Austin Ballard married, as well.

Hostage Situation—#27

Harlequin Intrigue–The Equalizers

Renee Vaughn went undercover to bring down a powerful drug lord. Finding her "in" to the reclusive criminal's life was easy—his brother Paul Reyes was his polar opposite. He was a classic good man in a bad situation—and the Equalizers' newest investigator was about to have her way with him. Finding themselves on the receiving end of a dirty double cross, Paul and Renee were running for their lives. As they joined forces to elude his brother's hired guns, their attraction grew deeper. But would it withstand Paul discovering the truth about who Renee really was? Who was being held hostage here—when both their hearts were put directly in harm's way?

Renee and Paul solve the case, revealing his ruthless brother. After a long, patient relationship, Paul asks Renee to marry him. They have recently had their first child, a beautiful little girl.

Colby vs. Colby—#28

Harlequin Intrigue–The Equalizers

With their reputations and Sunday dinner in jeopardy, Victoria Colby-Camp and her son, Jim, were at a standoff, and neither was about to give an inch when it came to Sam Johnson. He was Jim Colby's newest Equalizer, but a mystery to everyone else—until the past caught up with him and investigator Lisa Smith was called in to drag him back to the City of Angels to clear his name.

Hired by the Colby Agency, Lisa was by the book in every way, except when it came to Sam. After all this time, she couldn't forget him—and she had tried. With Sam framed for three gangland killings, Lisa found herself unraveling a man who trusted no one. But Sam would have to let Lisa in if they were ever going to expose a brutal killer before it was too late for the next victim…and the Colbys.

After an exhausting mission, Lisa moves to Chicago and is looking for a job with the Equalizers. She and Sam are married and expecting their first child.

Colby Rebuilt—#29

Harlequin Intrigue

Former U.S. marshal Shane Allen made one mistake on the job, and it cost him his reputation. Now he had a second chance, working an inside case for the newly rebuilt Colby Agency. And nothing, certainly not some tag-along woman, was going to ruin it.

After her sister's murder, Mary Jane Brooks wanted only justice. And Shane was crucial to nailing those responsible, even if he did send her pulse racing. Keeping things professional was downright impossible, especially when Mary Jane kept putting out conflicting signals. If Shane's instincts were right, this fragile beauty was a virgin in the worst kind of trouble—but was *he* ready to take it all away?

The Colby Agency has seen it all and was once nearly destroyed. But like the Phoenix, the Colby Agency is back! Shane and Mary Jane are married and have twin boys.

Guardian Angel—#30

Harlequin Intrigue

Who was the mysterious guardian angel? He'd succeeded where the FBI had failed, rescuing countless kidnapped children and bringing them to safety. His closely held hidden identity—as reclusive Nathan Tyler—was the only thing safeguarding his most private secrets. And they were about to go public.

Colby agent Anne Martin had a serial kidnapper on her hands and no viable leads. Except the Guardian Angel. Undisclosed liaisons with the vigilante weren't safe. The man was no saint, but neither was she. And breaking all the rules was only the first step they would take together.

With the case closed, Nathan and Ann return to his hometown and marry. With a toddler in diapers, they have just learned they are expecting baby number two!

Identity Unknown—#31

Harlequin Intrigue

Colby Agency's Patrick O'Brien knew only two things for sure: Sande Williams was a complete mystery and she was a woman in serious trouble. She was also gorgeous, but he wasn't about to put that in his internal report.

She'd woken up in a morgue—with toe tag and all! How could that happen, and why didn't she know who she was or where she'd come from? One by one the people associated with her were turning up dead. Was she an unwilling participant in an identity scheme or an accomplice? It was just the kind of case the Colby Agency took on—and just the kind of woman who could worm her way into Patrick's closed-off heart. But would he be next in her line for termination?

This is the first time the Colby Agency loses one of its own. RIP, Windy Millwood. During their time together, Sande finds out her true identity: Angela Tapley. The Colby Agency launches a new department focused on finding the lost, and Sande/Angela is brought on board for it. She and Patrick have married recently and are hoping to start a family soon.

Small-Town Secrets—#32

Harlequin Intrigue

Since 2000 the Colby Agency has taken on the most private of investigations. They now announce their Elite Reconnaissance Division: Our only mission—to find the missing! Chicago, Case Report #1.

Mission: Close a sixteen-year-old case—three teenage girls slain in a small Midwest town. Client: Dana Hall, twin sister of one of the victims. Troubled, amnesiac, alienated from family, suffering from horrific nightmares about the killer's identity. Investigator: William "Spence" Spencer. Thirty-six. Bachelor. Top-notch skills, on the job 24/7. Showed exceptional sensitivity to client's needs. Comments: Significant danger. Escalating threats against Dana's presence in town.

Spence believed Dana was hiding something relevant to the investigation. Possibly he might be hiding something himself. Had his strong, naturally protective nature compromised his professionalism? There was always a first time.

After a roller coaster of a ride, Dana and Spence go back to Chicago and decide to give their relationship a go. Wedding bells ring and a mere twelve months later the two welcome their first child.

The Bride's Secrets—#33

Harlequin Intrigue

Elite Reconnaissance Division: Our only mission—to find the missing! Chicago, Case Report #2.

Mission: Find a runaway bride. Expose her true identity. Target: Eve Mattson, self-described "problem solver" for hire. Had been on the wrong side of the law most of her life. Recently showed signs of putting the past behind her, especially after leaving the wrong guy at the altar. Investigator: J. T. Baxley, new employee who had mistaken his bride-to-be for an honest woman. Superior investigative skills, emotionally vulnerable, willing to take a bullet in the name of justice. Supervisor's comments: Twists and turns no one saw coming. Attraction again developing between Baxley and Mattson? Neither ever trusted anyone. Reports that the two have been spotted in passionate embraces in the midst of lethal situations.

When the bad guys are brought down, J.T. and Eve make some decisions. Despite their painful past and being thrown into a whirlwind investigation together, love has flourished once again. J.T. and Eve give their relationship another go and rush to the courthouse to make it official. A real family is in their immediate future.

His Secret Life—#34

Harlequin Intrigue

Elite Reconnaissance Division: Our only mission—to find the missing! Chicago, Case Report #3.

Mission: Find the hero who didn't want to be found. Client: A wealthy businessman who wouldn't rest until he repaid the man who saved his family from a car crash—and fled the scene. Investigator: Jane Sutton, former army counterintelligence officer, was the proverbial "plain Jane." Smart, tenacious, tough as nails, but longing for love. Didn't bargain for the danger that surrounded her target, Troy Benson…or her irresistible attraction to him. Supervisor's comments: On the lam from witness protection, Troy lives with a devastating secret from his past and trusts no one. Unwilling to let Jane help him reclaim his true identity. Reluctant to believe that what she really might find is the hero of her dreams.

With the case solved, Trace, aka Troy, and Jane let their relationship take its course. I am happy to report that the couple will be married this summer.

HQN Anthology

After a tragic mountain-climbing accident changed his life forever, NASCAR driver Jason Fewell hadn't been himself, on or off the track. So he headed into the wilderness to face his worst fears—and miraculously found the one woman who could make him whole again. If only she hadn't had secrets of her own.

After harrowing and treacherous climbs on the mountains and in their hearts, Molly and Jason follow their hearts to the finish line. The two are married and Molly is Jason's number one cheerleader as he wins race after race.

First Night—#36

Harlequin Intrigue

As far as Christmas packages went, Brandon Thomas was one surprisingly gorgeous surprise. And at the moment he was in over his too-handsome head. He'd showed up at the Colby Agency offices covered in blood and desperate for help unraveling a mystery of murder. Luckily for Brandon, Merri Walters was a determined investigator not about to let an innocent bystander get railroaded—especially so close to Christmas.

With careful coaxing, Merri learned that Brandon unknowingly possessed information high-level people wanted to keep secret. Now the only challenge was keeping Brandon at arm's length in order to make sure they both stayed alive to see the New Year.

Brandon and Merri fall head over heels in love and move in together. Wedding plans are under way! As a side note, Merri was also featured in two Bombshell books, *Silent Weapon* and *Silent Reckoning*.

Colby Lockdown—#37

Harlequin Intrigue

The Colby Agency of Chicago has long handled the most private investigations with discretion and success. Staff from the top down maintain pristine reputations and the agency always works within the law. Until now...

With a long list of clients came a few enemies. Someone wanted revenge—and was determined to get it, starting with Victoria Colby-Camp. The only hope for survival for Victoria and her staff lay with Colby investigator Slade Convoy and a total stranger—Mia Dawson, a personal assistant in the D.A.'s office.

With the offices in lockdown and holding hostages, the captors had one demand and a twenty-four-hour deadline: kidnap Cook County D.A. Gordon and deliver him to the Colby Agency. Slade's assignment was to gain the cooperation of Mia—the only person who knew how to get past Gordon's security—by whatever means necessary and bring in Gordon. Together Slade and Mia had no alternative but to break the law in order to execute the operation. But would they be able to plead their case once justice was served? And would the operation fail when Slade learned Mia had an agenda of her own?

In the end, Mia and Slade get through it all and begin a new relationship together. The two have just set a wedding date!

Colby Justice—#38

Harlequin Intrigue

With the deadline for his demands fast approaching, Victoria Colby-Camp's captor started to exact the revenge he deemed justice. Now in session: a mock trial sure to end in a death sentence for Victoria…unless Equalizer Ben Steele and Colby Agency rookie Penny Alexander could pull off a daring, nearly impossible rescue.

The only problem was some serious friction between the two. Loner Steele traveled with so much emotional baggage that he couldn't trust a woman partner. Alexander, new to the job and insecure, harbored a secret that could fatally jeopardize the mission. And once Steele found her out, anger, resentment, lies and accusations trailed their every heart-stopping move. Could this risk-all rescue operation—and the Colby Agency—be saved?

To start a new life with open minds and hearts, trusting the other, Ben and Penny begin a relationship!

Colby Control—#39

Harlequin Intrigue

When the Colby Agency and the Equalizers merged, their investigators and agents were expected to work together. But the moment Ted Tallant was teamed up with hotshot investigator Nora Friedman, there were sparks—and not the good kind. Nora was a risk taker, while Ted was a by-the-book kind of guy. When they were sent to Vegas on a case, those sparks turned into something hotter. They were good together—really good. But then an enemy from Nora's past twisted their assignment into something deadly, and all hell broke loose. Suddenly skill and attraction weren't enough. They would have to trust each other...or everyone would die.

Ted and Nora might have all but hated each other in the beginning, but things have changed! Nora has proposed to Ted and the two are going anywhere but Vegas for their nuptials.

Colby Velocity—#40

Harlequin Intrigue

Former Equalizer Leland "Rocky" Rockford did not have a problem working with Colby agent Kendra Todd. As far as he was concerned, partnering with her was one of the benefits of their agencies' merger. Something about her calm and composed air made him want to ruffle her feathers—until they were assigned to a murder case.

Fully in professional mode, Rocky was willing to do whatever necessary to support Kendra—and keep her safe. But as the case started cracking, so did the walls around her guarded heart. Now, with questions and bodies piling up, they had to outmaneuver the shadowy element that not only wanted them to fail, but wanted them dead....

As the case heats up, so does their attraction for one another. So when the case is closed, they take their relationship to the next level. A date has not been set, but don't be surprised if the two Colby investigators show up any day with matching gold bands.

Colby Brass—#41

Harlequin Intrigue

Five years ago they'd vowed to live separate lives…now they'd been brought together to complete their deadliest mission yet. As a Colby investigator, Trinity Barrett was one of the best at finding the missing and delivering justice. He hadn't confronted a challenge he couldn't handle with ease—until now. To locate an abducted child and bring her home safely, he must team up with Equalizer Evonne Cassidy…his ex-wife.

Launching a dangerous search in Chicago's underbelly was not Evonne's biggest obstacle—partnering with Trinity was. They'd managed to keep their history a secret, but in close quarters they couldn't deny the passion that still connected them. And if there was any hope for a Christmas reconciliation, they'd first have to survive their risky assignment.…

Evonne and Trinity's love is easily rekindled. At Victoria's insistence, they take some time off in a lovely cabin in Gatlinburg, Tennessee. Enough time to rekindle that old flame they have for each other. Lucas Camp has officially retired from the CIA and is now working side by side with Victoria.

Colby Core—#42

Harlequin Intrigue

More than just a Colby agent, he was the hero she'd been waiting for.… After years in captivity, waiting for a rescuer who never came, Tessa Woods met a mysterious stranger who was determined to help bring down a human-trafficking ring and save the other victims…including her child. But could she put all her dreams of a Merry Christmas into the hands of a handsome stranger?

Colby agent Riley Porter thought being a former SEAL had prepared him for anything. When he went undercover to find Tessa, he didn't expect his professional mission to become personal. Yet caring for the brave, passionate woman who was ready to risk her life to end an evil cycle was far beyond his control. As the danger escalated, Riley had to convince Tessa to do the impossible for their own survival—trust him to protect her.

Tessa's hero finally came! She and Riley are a couple now and raising her little girl.

Missing—#43

Harlequin Intrigue—The New Equalizers

"I need your help. Please." And with those words, tough guy Jonathan Foley melted. It had been years since he'd seen the only woman to climb his wall of solitude…months since he'd joined an elite team of operatives called the Equalizers and hidden away his secrets. But now Melissa Shepherd needed him—and there was no denying her.

Melissa's niece was missing and she knew only Jonathan could see past the lies in her small Alabama hometown and find Polly. Searching alongside the man she'd loved and lost would prove difficult…and downright dangerous. But she'd have to—because for the little girl, time was running out….

Jonathan Foley resigned as an Equalizer and moved to Alabama to be with Melissa. The two had a whirlwind marriage and are finally truly happy.

Colby Damaged—#44

Harlequin Intrigue—The New Equalizers

"I'm no hero." It was supposed to be a simple assignment—follow a woman. As an operative with the elite team of Equalizers, Dakota Garrett had faced hell and lived without any new baggage. So why was he left with dead bodies, a kidnap victim and a damsel in distress on his latest assignment?

Wannabe Colby agent Lucky Malone was in over her head. Only the dark stranger could save her and her kidnapped boss, the esteemed Victoria Colby-Camp, but like Lucky, Dakota had demons that haunted him, a past that shadowed him. And this case forced him to meet his biggest fear head-on. Lucky would give anything to help the man she'd come to love, but her fate was in Dakota's hands. Could he play the role he'd always avoided—hero?

Dakota Garrett leaves the Equalizers but stays in Chicago with Lucky. He has just bought the ring and is planning a special moment to pop the question!

Colby Broken—#45

Harlequin Intrigue—The New Equalizers

"That stranger…is my wife." After seven years of agony, Linc Reece was certain he'd found his dead wife—alive and living in a tiny Tennessee town. He was sure Mia Grant *was* Lori, the wife he'd lost in an undercover case gone bad. Now the operative for the elite team of Equalizers had to prove it… even if he had to kidnap her.

Mia Grant saw the hope in Linc's eyes…but just because she liked the scent of vanilla, blues and old houses didn't make her his long-lost wife. Nothing about him was familiar, except the sizzle she felt when they touched. But when they discovered Lori's records destroyed and her photos stolen, even Mia knew someone had gone to great lengths to make her forget. And the man she had trusted most would do anything to ensure she never remembered….

Reece leaves the Equalizers to rebuild his life. Mia/Lori realizes she loves Linc no matter if she never remembers the life they once shared. She wants to be a part of the new life he is building. They renew their vows and are planning to have their first child.

Colby Classified—#46

Harlequin Intrigue

"Who are you?" Colby Agency investigator Levi Stark had been prepared for the worst when his boss sent him to find her agency's deadliest enemy. But deep undercover in a Mexican mining outpost, Levi met danger from the unlikeliest source—an unknown blonde spitfire on the same trail.

Casey Manning had been secretly sent by Levi's boss's husband, Lucas Camp. The benched CIA agent trusted no one and worked alone…until she and Levi found themselves outmanned and outgunned. Around her sexy new partner, Casey had a feeling that protecting her identity—and her heart—would prove tougher than keeping them safe from the Colbys' most wanted….

After facing certain death together and overcoming it, Casey and Levi are an item! Their wedding plans are under way, with Casey's uncle, the enigmatic Thomas Casey, and his close friend Lucas Camp advising the young couple.

Decoded—#47

Harlequin Intrigue

"Who are you?" Slade Keaton was the man Maggie James
fell in love with…until she learned that everything she knew
about him was a lie. Escaping a hit meant for him, she found
herself on the run—fleeing a danger she couldn't comprehend
with a man she couldn't trust. And pregnant with his baby.

Though he'd had dozens of aliases, Slade couldn't forget who he was—the son of a merciless assassin named the
Dragon. He'd kept out of his mother's reach for years till a
Colby Agency investigator put him—and Maggie—on her
radar. Now could Slade become the very thing he hated in
order to save the woman and child he loved?

After years on the run and in hiding, Slade Keaton (birth
name: Tripp Marek) can be free to live a normal life and
no longer have to look over his shoulder. Thirty years ago
Lucas Camp and the Dragon had a relationship, and Slade is
the result of that affair! He is offered a position at the Colby
Agency. He accepts and closes the Equalizers. Any and all of
his employees are welcome to join the Colby Agency. Victoria and Lucas announce their retirement and the opening of a
new Colby branch in Texas. Keaton buys a house in Chicago
and proposes to Maggie…she says yes!

Colby Law—#48

Harlequin Intrigue

Lyle McCaleb was eager to begin work for the Colby Agency when their Houston office opened. His first case involved a twenty-two-year-old murder case the world had presumed closed until Rafe Barker, the Princess Killer, currently in his last thirty days of death row, revealed that his three daughters (assumed to be his and his wife's final victims) were alive and well and in need of protection. His wife, Clare, the other half of the Princess Killer team, had recently been released and Rafe swore she wanted to find their daughters and do what was supposed to have been done all those years ago.

The case took Lyle to the last place he expected to go— Copperas Cove, Texas, and his first love, Sadie Gilmore. Sadie was a stubborn young woman who had a deeply tender spot for animals. She owned and operated Second Chance Ranch outside Copperas Cove, where she rescued rodeo horses. She had no idea that she was really Sarah Barker, the youngest of the Barker children. Could Lyle convince her to allow him to protect her before it was too late?

High Noon—#49

Harlequin Intrigue

The hunt for Clare Barker and the truth continued. This time it was the middle daughter, Laney Seagers (formerly Lisa Barker), and her son in need of protection. As a single mother Laney had her hands full running the High Noon saloon and raising Buddy, her precocious son. It wasn't bad enough that the bank was nipping at her heels and her son's father had decided to cause her trouble, but then a stranger showed up with an unbelievable story. Laney wasn't who she thought she was—and her biological mother might be trying to kill her.

Joel Hayden didn't want to tell Laney about her disturbing family secret until absolutely necessary, but that moment came all too soon. The danger closed in way too fast and little Buddy went missing. Lucas Camp arrived as backup and was caught in the cross fire. Rafe Barker continued taunting Victoria with clues that made no sense.

The Colby Agency was the best…but could they find the truth before someone else died?

Colby Roundup—#50

Harlequin Intrigue

Olivia Westfield (aka Elizabeth Barker) was the oldest and the only one of the three Barker girls who knew she was adopted. She was dead set on finding the truth about Rafe and Clare Barker. Could the man who was her biological father and who had been labeled pure evil actually be innocent? Or was Clare, her mother, the real victim here?

Russell "Russ" St. James had been assigned to watch after Olivia without interfering in her life. But how long would it be before the risk was too great to her for him not to intercede? And when he did step in, would it be too late? Olivia took that choice out of his hands by confronting him. The two dived into an Olympic-size pool of deadly deceptions that threatened to drown all involved in the investigation.

The Barker girls are safe and Rafe's sentence will be carried out for his heinous deeds. Clare's name has been cleared. She will require years of counseling, but she wants a relationship with her daughters and they are agreeable to taking things one step at a time. Victoria and Lucas have decided to take retirement a little more seriously.

Sadie and Lyle are the first to marry, with her adopted father escorting her down the aisle. Joel and Laney are making plans for wedding number two. Buddy adores Joel! Olivia has returned to law school. She and Russ will be exchanging vows as soon as she graduates. The sisters are enjoying getting to know each other.

* * * * *

Look for more Colby Agency books
coming from Harlequin Intrigue!

#1365 GAGE
The Lawmen of Silver Creek Ranch
Delores Fossen
After faking his death to protect his family, CIA agent Gage Ryland is forced to secretly return from the grave to save his ex, Lynette Herrington, who's carrying a secret of her own.

#1366 SECRET ASSIGNMENT
Cooper Security
Paula Graves
On a visit to a private island, an archivist stumbles onto an invasion, forcing her to work with the handsome caretaker to learn who will stop at nothing to gain access to the island—and why.

#1367 KANSAS CITY COWBOY
The Precinct: Task Force
Julie Miller
Sheriff Boone Harrison and police psychologist Kate Kilpatrick couldn't be more different. But trusting each other is the only way to catch a killer...and find a second chance at love.

#1368 MOMMY MIDWIFE
Cassie Miles
Nine months after a night she'll never forget, a pregnant midwife must trust the baby's father, a man she barely knows, to rescue her from the madman who wants her baby.

#1369 COPY THAT
HelenKay Dimon
A girl-next-door gets sucked into a dangerous new life when a wounded border patrol agent lands on her doorstep, with gunmen hot on his trail.

#1370 HER COWBOY AVENGER
Thriller
Kerry Connor
Her husband's murder turned her into an outcast and a suspect—and the only man who can help her is the tall, dark cowboy she thought she'd never see again.

REQUEST YOUR FREE BOOKS!
2 FREE NOVELS PLUS 2 FREE GIFTS!

Harlequin®

INTRIGUE®

BREATHTAKING ROMANTIC SUSPENSE

YES! Please send me 2 FREE Harlequin Intrigue® novels and my 2 FREE gifts (gifts are worth about $10). After receiving them, if I don't wish to receive any more books, I can return the shipping statement marked "cancel." If I don't cancel, I will receive 6 brand-new novels every month and be billed just $4.49 per book in the U.S. or $5.24 per book in Canada. That's a saving of at least 14% off the cover price! It's quite a bargain! Shipping and handling is just 50¢ per book in the U.S. and 75¢ per book in Canada.* I understand that accepting the 2 free books and gifts places me under no obligation to buy anything. I can always return a shipment and cancel at any time. Even if I never buy another book, the two free books and gifts are mine to keep forever.

182/382 HDN FEQ2

Name	(PLEASE PRINT)
Address	Apt. #
City	State/Prov.	Zip/Postal Code

Signature (if under 18, a parent or guardian must sign)

Mail to the **Reader Service:**
IN U.S.A.: P.O. Box 1867, Buffalo, NY 14240-1867
IN CANADA: P.O. Box 609, Fort Erie, Ontario L2A 5X3

Not valid for current subscribers to Harlequin Intrigue books.

**Are you a subscriber to Harlequin Intrigue books
and want to receive the larger-print edition?
Call 1-800-873-8635 or visit www.ReaderService.com.**

* Terms and prices subject to change without notice. Prices do not include applicable taxes. Sales tax applicable in N.Y. Canadian residents will be charged applicable taxes. Offer not valid in Quebec. This offer is limited to one order per household. All orders subject to credit approval. Credit or debit balances in a customer's account(s) may be offset by any other outstanding balance owed by or to the customer. Please allow 4 to 6 weeks for delivery. Offer available while quantities last.

Your Privacy—The Reader Service is committed to protecting your privacy. Our Privacy Policy is available online at www.ReaderService.com or upon request from the Reader Service.

We make a portion of our mailing list available to reputable third parties that offer products we believe may interest you. If you prefer that we not exchange your name with third parties, or if you wish to clarify or modify your communication preferences, please visit us at www.ReaderService.com/consumerschoice or write to us at Reader Service Preference Service, P.O. Box 9062, Buffalo, NY 14269. Include your complete name and address.

HI11B

CINDY DEES

takes you on a wild journey to find the truth
in her new miniseries

Code X

Aiden McKay is more than just an ordinary man. As part of
an elite secret organization, Aiden was genetically enhanced
to increase his lung capacity and spend extended time under
water. He is a committed soldier, focused and dedicated
to his job. But when Aiden saves impulsive free spirit
Sunny Jordan from drowning she promptly overturns his
entire orderly, solitary world.

As the danger creeps closer, Adien soon realizes Sunny is the
target…but can he save her in time?

Breathless Encounter

Find out this August!

plus
**BONUS
STORY
INSIDE!**

Look out for a reader-favorite bonus story included in each
Harlequin Romantic Suspense book this August!

www.Harlequin.com

HRS27786

Werewolf and elite U.S. Navy SEAL, Matt Parker, must set aside his prejudices and partner with beautiful Fae Sienna McClare to find a magic orb that threatens to expose the secret nature of his entire team.

Harlequin® Nocturne presents the debut of beloved author Bonnie Vanak's new miniseries, PHOENIX FORCE.

Enjoy a sneak preview of THE COVERT WOLF, available August 2012 from Harlequin® Nocturne.

Sienna McClare was Fae, accustomed to open air and fields. Not this boxy subway car.

As the oily smell of fear clogged her nostrils, she inhaled deeply, tried thinking of tall pines waving in the wind, the chatter of birds and a deer cropping grass. A wolf watching a deer, waiting. Prey. Images of fangs flashing, tearing, wet sounds…

No!

She fought the panic freezing her blood. And was gradually able to push the fear down into a dark spot deep inside her. The stench of Draicon werewolf clung to her like cheap perfume.

Sienna hated glamouring herself as a Draicon werewolf, but it was necessary if she was going to find the Orb of Light. Someone had stolen the Orb from her colony, the Los Lobos Fae. A Draicon who'd previously been seen in the area was suspected. Sienna had eagerly seized the chance to help when asked because finding it meant she would no longer be an outcast. The Fae had cast her out when she turned twenty-one because she was the bastard child of a sweet-faced Fae and a Draicon killer. But if she found the Orb, Sienna could return to the only home she'd known. It also meant she could recover her lost memories.

Every time she tried searching for her past, she met with a closed door. Who was she? Which side ruled her?

Fae or Draicon?

Draicon, no way in hell.

Sensing someone staring, she glanced up, saw a man across the aisle. He was heavily muscled and radiated power and confidence. Yet he also had the face of a gentle warrior. Sienna's breath caught. She felt a stir of sexual chemistry.

He was as lonely and grief stricken as she was. Her heart twisted. Who had hurt this man? She wanted to go to him, comfort him and ease his sorrow. Sienna smiled.

An odd connection flared between them. Sienna locked her gaze to his, desperately needing someone who understood.

Then her nostrils flared as she caught his scent. Hatred boiled to the surface. Not a man. Draicon.

The enemy.

Find out what happens next in THE COVERT WOLF by Bonnie Vanak.

Available August 2012 from Harlequin® Nocturne wherever books are sold.

Harlequin Super Romance®

Enjoy a month of compelling, emotional stories, including a poignant new tale of love lost and found from

Sarah Mayberry

When Angela Bartlett loses her best friend to a rare heart condition, it seems only natural that she step in and help widower and friend Michael Young. The last thing she expects is to find herself falling for him....

Within Reach

Available August 7!

HARLEQUIN
RECOMMENDED
Read!

"I loved it. I thought the story was very believable.
The characters were endearing. The author wrote beautifully...
I will be looking for future books by Sarah Mayberry."

—Sherry, Harlequin® Superromance® reader, on *Her Best Friend*

Find more great stories this month from
Harlequin® Superromance® at

www.Harlequin.com

HSRSM71795